**Guilty. Hopeless. ~~Con~~**
**Everything change~~d~~**

# FACE ~~T~~
# WI~~TH~~
# FORGIVENESS

## A look at the Saviour of second chances.

# KAY D. RIZZO

**Pacific Press Publishing Association**
Nampa, Idaho
Oshawa, Ontario, Canada

Edited by Jerry D. Thomas
Cover illustration by Bryant Eastman
Cover and inside design by Dennis Ferree

Rizzo, Kay D., 1943-
    Face to face with forgiveness : a look at the saviour
of second chances / Kay D. Rizzo.
        p.    cm.
    ISBN 0-8163-1366-0  (pbk. : alk. paper)
    1. Mary Magdalene, Saint. 2. Bible. N. T.—History
of Biblical events.    3.  Christian women saints—
Palestine.    4.  Biographical. gsafd.  5.  Christian.
lcsh.  I.  Title.
PS3568.I836C38   1997
813'.54—DC20                        96-43771
                                    CIP
                                    Rev.

97 98 99 00 01 • 5 4 3 2 1

To Kelli Wheeler,

my daughter,
my friend, and my confidante.

Zephaniah 3:17 (Living Bible)

# CONTENTS

# INTRODUCTION

*"They drew a circle that shut me out*
*—heretic, rebel, a thing to flout—*
*but love and I had the wit to win.*
*We drew a circle that took them in."*
(Edwin Markham "Outwitted")

Outcast! Being excluded from the community is never easy. Before he became Kentucky's hero, Daniel Boone and his family were shunned by the little Pennsylvania community of Ephrata and forced to leave. Anne Hutchinson and her family would not have been massacred in the wilds of Rhode Island if they'd not been banished from Massachusetts Bay Colony.

In the *Outcasts of Poker Flats*, the nineteenth century American writer Bret Hart wrote about a group of people forced to flee from the good townsfolk's righteous wrath during a prairie blizzard. Huddled together in an abandoned cabin with no wood for the fireplace and no food to eat, each one of this ragtag group—the riffraff of frontier society—tells his or her story as they fight to stay alive.

I first read the tale from a high school literature anthology. Unlike many of the stories I read during my

7

adolescence, this one stayed with me. I still think about it occasionally. I wonder about the outcasts in our society today. Is it much different for them than it was for frontier Americans? For first century ne'er-do-wells, in fact?

What is it like to be a social outcast? Like most teens, I knew how it felt to be snubbed, to feel unaccepted by the "in" crowd. At one time or another, each of us has felt the slight of social snobbery. Sometimes one is made an outcast by his sins; sometimes by accident of birth.

My sister-in-law remembers growing up in Brooklyn, New York, in the thirties and forties and being the only Italian child in school. In the fifties, I grew up as a Protestant English girl in a primarily Irish-Catholic neighborhood. Today, my African-American friend Terry Johnson encounters racism in many of the places he goes.

Racial, ethnic, economic, cultural, social, and sexual barriers always hurt the one on the outside, whether by accident or design. However, the barriers hurt the ones on the inside too. These walls isolate and imprison them in a very narrow way of thinking and living.

Jesus came to tear down these barriers. He came to establish a new kingdom where one's race, one's gender, one's social status dissolves in the wash of His love, a place where one's past is forgiven and forgotten. Jesus said, "The Spirit . . . has anointed me to preach good news to the poor . . . to proclaim freedom for the prisoners . . . to release the oppressed . . ." (Luke 4:18, NIV).

In other words, He came to rescue the "outcasts of Galilee's Flats."

No story better illustrates the success of the Saviour's

mission than does the story of Mary, the fallen woman, the prostitute, the demon-possessed. Mary Magdalene has become the most commonly used exemplar when referring to sin. Magdalene, written with a small "m," in several languages has come to mean a reformed prostitute.

More importantly to you and to me, Mary's story reveals the face of a loving Saviour, a Saviour who patiently forgives again and again—casting out the demons seven times if necessary.

The number seven has a special significance in God's Word as well as in the civilizations surrounding ancient Israel—advanced civilizations like Greece and Egypt. Symbolically, the number seven seems to express a complete period of time, the idea of totality itself.

Mary's repeated forgiveness also reveals the sympathetic side of the Master as He deals with society's outcasts. The story touches each of us, whether we are outcasts by birth or by our own ugly sins.

Scholars disagree on the identity of Mary. Some say Mary Magdalene and Mary of Bethany were the same woman, as well as the woman thrown at Jesus' feet. Others believe these women are three separate individuals. Some indicate there may have been as many as seven Marys, including the mother of Jesus. The name *Mary* in Hebrew (*mirjam*) means "to be loved." In Aramaic, *Mary (marjam)* means "lady." With both of these languages being commonly spoken in Jesus' day, "Mary" was a common name to hear.

For the sake of the message in this book, I am assuming Mary Magdalene and Mary, the sister of Martha and Lazarus, to be one individual.

# FACE TO FACE WITH FORGIVENESS

*Face to Face With Forgiveness* is not meant to be a definitive tome on biblical history. Neither is it an exegesis on Jesus and the women's liberation movement. It was written, however, to give us a fresh look at the face of the Saviour through a fallen woman's eyes. Besides, what woman among us cannot relate to the temptations of the senses, the hunger to be loved, and the pain of rejection.

Come walk with me as we find ourselves in the story of Mary, the woman who loved too much, as she encounters the Man whose love knew no limits.

# FACE TO FACE WITH FORGIVENESS

# *Section*
# 1

# Mary, the Sinner

# CAUGHT IN THE ACT!

*" 'Teacher, this woman was caught*
*in the act of adultery' "*
(John 8:4, NIV).

Caught in the act! From the moment the church elders burst into her home, Mary knew she was a dead woman. There would be no defense attorney pleading her case, no evidence of extenuating circumstances submitted, no tender mercy extended to soften the hard-edge of justice. The Law of Moses left no room for negotiation or interpretation. She'd been caught in the act of adultery. She knew her fate.

Caught in the act! The woman searched for a hint of compassion in the cold, harsh faces surrounding her adulterous bed. No one moved to come to her defense. Instead, her accusers—many her former customers—tried to outshout each other to camouflage their own complicity. For courage, she reached out to grasp the hand of the "john" lying on the bed beside her. All she found was a rumpled sheet. Her partner in passion had fled, vanishing just after the "morality swat team" arrived.

Caught in the act. As the truth of her situation unfolded in her brain, terror welled up within her. It was a setup. She should have known. From the unusual early morning encounter by the village well to the impatient pawing to the sudden intrusion—a setup. But for what purpose? It didn't make sense to her.

Mary had always been fair in her dealings. She'd never cheated her customers of her favors or snatched their coin purses when they weren't looking as some whores on the strip did. She'd earned every shekel they'd paid her. Questions swam in her befuddled brain. Why? Why would they betray her now?

One of the men grabbed the frightened woman's hair and yanked her from the bed. Another tossed her a robe and the command, "Cover yourself, slut!"

She cast a jaundiced eye at her dubious benefactor; a slight curl forming at one corner of her lips. What a radical change in tone from the promises of pleasure he'd panted in her ear a few evenings ago. Their eyes met for an instant. His face reddened; then he turned toward the leader of the pack. "We're wasting time. Let's get out of here."

Helpless, she fumbled to fasten the belt of the robe about her waist. Hands like bone-crushing tentacles groped her, squeezed and bruised her arms and body. They dragged her from the room. Trapped between two of the men, Mary stumbled down the stone staircase. At one point, she lost her balance and fell to one knee.

"Get to your feet, woman!" The town's leading Pharisee yanked her forward by her hair. She struggled to break free, but the brown muscular hands gripping her upper arms tightened their grasp. Someone slapped her face, bruising her left cheek and blackening her eye. Another slap across the face and blood spurted from her broken lip.

Caught in the act. Where were they taking her? To the town square? To the temple courtyard? Were her executioners already gathering the stones that would end her life? Her head throbbed with a thousand unanswered questions.

Bruising her bare feet on the pebbles in the road, she again fell to her knees. "Please, help me. Please," she cried, calling out the name of one of the men whom she'd known for many years. The man on her left yanked her by the arm, nearly wrenching it out of its socket. She screamed in pain. They ignored her cries and continued dragging her through the dust like a limp rag doll. Tears ran down her cheeks while blood and dirt filled her mouth. She bit down on something hard then spit out a piece of a tooth.

The Law of Moses demanded that both of the guilty parties caught in adultery be stoned. But that detail of the law her accusers had conveniently ignored.

The law also required that it be the adulterer's husband's duty to bring charges against his philandering wife. The actions of the accusers were totally unauthorized. But these men were in no mood to quibble over detail. Their agenda didn't include justice or adherence to the law.

At one point, when she raised her head begging for mercy, she caught a glimpse of her morning's customer, haunting the peripheral of the crowd. She understood the difference between the letter of the law and the reality of the law. She didn't try to deceive herself regarding society's double standard for men and for women. She would die, and he would go free to proposition again.

Caught in the act. All along she'd known the end result of the lifestyle she lived. Family members and friends lost no opportunity to regularly remind her of her fate—that is, those family members and friends who hadn't long since deserted her. Now the day had come. Now she could expect the worst—death by stoning according to the Law of Moses. Now she would face her executioners: helpless . . . hopeless . . . defenseless . . . friendless . . . alone.

Being alone when in trouble is truly being alone. Though the crowd was peppered with guilt, no one stepped forward to share her fate. When sympathy was needed most, it was not there. The world is no different today than it was in Jesus' day. When a worker is being censured for a real or imagined "sin," others steer clear of their compatriot, often adding painful barbs and suspicions to the original accusations in order to *fend off* any doubts of their own loyalty. And Mary? What could she say? How could she deny her guilt? She'd been caught in the act.

Caught in the act. A few minutes before the end of my classroom's lunch hour play time, I returned to my classroom for the whistle I'd accidentally left behind. That's when I noticed that the lock on the storage-room door had been rifled. Someone had torn open one of the fund-raising boxes and stolen several of the candy bars.

I was horrified! As a twenty-something-year-old teacher, I couldn't imagine any of my young charges doing such a thing.

## Caught in the Act

I marched to the playground and blew the whistle, announcing the end of recess. The children scrambled to fall into line. The younger ones jostled one another to be at the head of the line. As I counted heads, I realized that three of my bigger boys—Mike, Gary, and Andy—were missing. I gazed across the empty playground. The three boys were nowhere to be seen. I turned to Mike's younger sister.

"Where's your brother?" I asked. She shrugged, her eyes widened in claimed ignorance.

I turned to another child. "Jerry, have you seen Andy or Gary?" The boy shrugged as well.

I gazed at the upturned faces before me. "No one knows where Mike, Gary, or Andy have gone?"

I got the same reaction from the rest of my class shrugs and a bevy of denials. Like the character in Shakespeare's *Romeo and Juliet*, I mumbled under my breath, "Me thinks thou dost protest too much."

I felt a tug on my skirt. I looked down to find Linda, the tiniest of my first graders, trying to get my attention. "Teacher, teacher," she whispered. "I saw them out behind the storage shed."

Several of the children nearest Linda growled their displeasure. "Tattletale!" someone hissed.

I straightened my shoulders and faced the group. Apparently, the expression on my face betrayed my feelings. The students were suddenly silent. "Listen carefully," I said. "While I search for Mike, Gary, and Andy, I want you to stand right where you are. In line! No talking. No pushing. Don't move! Do you understand?"

The solemn faces nodded. What else could they do with that look on my face?

"I mean it. Don't move an inch," I repeated.

Pulling my jangled nerves into line, I marched behind the metal equipment shed, where I found my three errant boys, their faces and hands stained with guilt and melted chocolate. The foil from the discarded candy wrappers glinted in the sun beside them.

My hands on my hips, I towered over their frightened forms. "What is the big idea?"

Before either of the others could reply, Andy leapt to his feet. "I didn't do nothin', Mrs. Kay, I didn't do nothin'. Gary and Mike gave me some of their chocolate, and I ate it, that's all. I didn't want to eat it, but they made me."

Caught in the act. Andy had been caught in the act, chocolate stains on his shirt, fingers and face, almonds shards between his teeth, a half-eaten bar resting in his lap.

"Andy! What am I going to do with you?" I turned my back for a moment, fighting to swallow my grin. He reminded me of a cartoon I'd once seen. In the "Garfield" strip, Jon had caught Garfield with one paw in the fishbowl and a goldfish tail sticking out of his mouth. Garfield's response was, "Jon, it's not what you think."

Caught in the act. We live in a world of excuses, an atmosphere of denial of responsibility for our own actions. We blame the other guy. If my child fails math, it's the teacher's fault. If a thief breaks his leg while trying to burglarize my home, he sues me for the damage. If a murderer is found with a smoking gun in his hand and standing over a fresh corpse, his lawyer blames the culprit's abusive parents. Even when caught in the act, from stolen candy bars to murder, the guilty deny their guilt.

But Mary didn't deny her guilt. She knew better than to blame the "johns" for her sin. What was the use? She'd been caught in the act. It had become evident that none of her lovers would defend her. No one would utter a word of comfort. No man would step forward. No woman would wrap a warm blanket of compassion about her shoulders to cover her shivering, body.

The prostitute found herself on that fateful afternoon shivering . . . exposed . . . alone.

# CHAPTER TWO

# THE MAN CALLED JESUS

*"At dawn he appeared again in the temple courts,
where all the people gathered around him,
and he sat down to teach them."*
(John 8:20, NIV)

The Man called Jesus sat on the marble steps of the temple, surrounded by a swarm of eager, curious people, demanding He speak to them of the kingdom of God— the kingdom He would form to defeat the hated Roman army. They surrounded Him, circles within circles, each with his own thoughts, each with his own agenda, each with his own motives.

In the outer circle, the Pharisees and their priestly brigade stood with arms folded, their lips turned upward at the corners, for they knew the future. "He preaches as if He is the Messiah," one religious leader hissed.

"Imagine! The Messiah coming from Galilee," another whispered, dismissing the Man with a flick of the wrist. "Anyone who knows Scripture will tell you that the Messiah will come from David's village, from

Bethlehem, not Nazareth!"

A temple policeman overheard the exchange. The officer edged closer. "Say what you will, but I've never heard any man speak like this Man."

The elder of the two lordly Pharisees glared. "Are you carried away like the rest of this rabble?"

The policeman quailed under the Pharisee's censure, shaking his head and mumbling something innocuous.

The Pharisee curled his lip. "You don't see any of the religious teachers believing in Him, do you? Or any of the Pharisees? It's only this crowd, ignorant of God's law, that is taken in by Him—and damned for it!"

The second Pharisee shot a furtive glance over his shoulder then snickered. "Don't worry. In a few minutes you'll see the upstart finally put in His place. After today, you wait, you'll see. No one will listen to a word He says, miracles or not."

Women clutching the hands of their young children populated the second concentric circle, except for the few children who'd dared to brave the censure of the crowd by pressing next to Jesus. The mothers would have pressed closer to the Teacher as well, but they knew their place. However, even within their socially assigned ranks, they jostled one another for position.

The men of the community occupied the third and the closest circle to the Teacher, except for the Teacher's disciples surrounding Him.

The Man from Galilee held a young child on His lap— a little girl of perhaps five or six years old. A second child, a boy of the same age, leaned up against the Teacher's arm. And a third, a boy of ten, sat at His feet, staring with awe at the Man. The Teacher spoke with the children for a few minutes.

The adults strained to hear His words. From the back row, the religious leaders frowned at the joyous laughter coming from the children and from the Rabbi.

"This is a church, sacred ground," one scribe sputtered. "Doesn't He realize such frivolity is inappropriate in God's house?" Their frowns deepened when they noted the children's young faces glowing with pleasure. "Why does He waste His time with young children? That's women's work!" they murmured. The Teacher's disciples were wondering the same question.

Then, as if He'd read the thoughts of the restive crowd, the Master Teacher lifted His eyes toward the adults. "You ask me to speak of the kingdom of God . . ." Jesus paused. His gaze swept across the audience. "The kingdom of God is like a . . ."

The roar of an angry mob approaching the courtyard drowned out His words. Like children on a playground, the crowd turned their heads and craned their necks to see what was happening, their fickle attention diverted to a more sensational show. When the procession rounded the corner and came into view, a shiver of excitement skittered through the assembly. Even as the people parted to make way for the company of Pharisees, the smell of violence filled the air.

A murmur of satisfaction and carnal delight followed the glimpses of bruised flesh, torn silk, and matted hair being dragged through the dust. The situation spoke for itself. The temple scribes and priests in the outer ring assessed the situation instantly and began searching for the best rocks to heave at the victim.

The leader of the brigade bullied his way forward. A

robe of self-satisfaction covered his rotund body. The two men who'd been dragging the woman thrust her into the center of the circle, forcing her to stand before her executioners. She swayed. No hand reached out to steady her.

The crowd stared, salivating with horror and expectation. Blood dribbled from the woman's mouth onto the twisted lapel of her stained silken robe, a robe that only partially covered her bruised body. Tongues clicked, noses snorted, and more than a few grunted with pleasure.

Mothers pressed the faces of their children to their bosoms, protecting them from viewing the unsightly woman. The children who'd been close to Jesus quailed in fear. Condemnation passed through the crowd, growing in volume, until the hateful words ricocheted off the marble walls surrounding the courtyard.

"Slut!"

"Harlot."

"Filth!"

"Time to clean up the neighborhood."

"Get a rock!"

Through swollen and blackened eyes, the disheveled woman stared at the dust-covered feet of her accusers. Some wore the sandals of fishermen. The town's aristocracy wore the expensive imported leather from Persia. Then there were the sandals of the town's respectable housewives, their hand-beaded sandals and their cries of vengeance.

"Trash!"

". . . shouldn't be around respectable women."

Bitter words oozing with toxic hate. Insults hurled.

The stoning of Mary had begun, verbal stones from former friends, neighbors, lovers. Stones that were meant to sting, to wound, to destroy the soul before they attacked the body.

Have you ever felt like Mary? Hurting from the censure of a carefully contrived slur? Perhaps you can still feel the pain it left. An injury that appeared out of the blue, from someone you cared about. A sarcastic barb, a harsh slip of the tongue, a put-down. Leaving bruised feelings, injured pride, and a broken heart.

Old or new, recent or ancient history, your wound is still painful to the touch. The scar tissue is thin and vulnerable to the slightest irritation. It hurts today as badly as it did the day you received it. You can understand the pain Mary felt as she stood surrounded by her neighbors. Deserved or undeserved, pain is still pain. Hurt still hurts.

Mary's face burned with each fiery jeer. The accused woman's long tangled hair, once her pride and joy, was now matted with blood and grit. Mercifully, it fell forward over her shoulders to hide her shame and embarrassment.

A hand shoved her forward. She jerked to a stop inches from the sandals of the master miracle worker, Jesus. She recognized the hem of His garment—she'd watched Him from afar. She'd seen Him give sight to the blind. She'd heard how He healed the paralytic. And how He had reached out and touched the unclean hand of the leper.

Mary saw herself as a leper. Unclean. What would it be like to be clean again? To once more be a virgin? To wear the innocence of a child? Whenever she thought of the Miracle Worker, she speculated. Could He . . . ? Would He . . . ?

She had longed to approach Him, but she dared not— not a Man so pure, so filled with goodness and selfless love. From afar, she'd seen Him disembark from His friends' fishing boats. She'd watched the children run to His waiting arms. She'd seen Him sweep a child into the air and twirl about on the sand. She'd watched Him admire a child's partially constructed sand castle. She'd seen Him kiss the bruise on a child's elbow.

A desire welled up within her, the desire to be a child again, innocent and free. If only she could run into His waiting arms. If only she could hear His words of comfort and encouragement.

If only . . . if only . . . if only . . . Her life had been a series of "if onlys." If only she had listened to her sister about being so friendly. If only the Pharisee hadn't seen the twelve-year-old girl drawing water from the town well that day. If only she hadn't listened to his compliments as he lured her to his estate. If only she could find that little lost girl.

Thousands of days had passed since then, a lifetime of days. Each day of living and each night of passion had dragged her closer to this fate-filled moment. The young woman sighed, her shoulders drooping even farther. She'd been caught in the act. She had nowhere to turn. She must accept her fate.

# CHAPTER THREE

# FACE TO FACE

*" 'In the Law Moses commanded*
*us to stone such women' "*
(John 8:5, NIV).

The temple leaders thrust the woman forward. She found herself face to face with Jesus. Face to face. This wasn't the way Mary had imagined meeting the promised Messiah. She'd considered searching for Him in the night. She would offer to serve Him in the best way she knew how, the only way she knew.

Somehow, even as she imagined her encounter with the Man, Jesus, she knew He was like no other man. He wouldn't want to take advantage of her, to slake His selfish desires. No, this Man reached out to meet other peoples' needs instead of His own. He wouldn't want what other men wanted of her. Staring into the night, she would ask herself again and again, "What would He want from me?"

But now, it was too late. Thrust into the center of a condemning mob, surrounded and going down for the count, she realized she would never know the Teacher and what He might be able to do for her. Her shoulders sagged with resignation. Her eyes swam with tears. She clutched her torn bodice to her breast, a feeble attempt at decency. She stared down at her own bloody and dirt-encrusted feet.

There would be no second chances—no mercy. The crowd wouldn't allow mercy. She had nowhere to run. Mary found herself face to face with the Man who had become her Judge and Jury. Face to face with Truth.

Are you standing where Mary stood that day, staring into the mirror of Truth? Perhaps you've been condemned because of your own sins. Perhaps, by the sins of others or just because of sin itself.

When the doctor utters the diagnosis, "uterine cancer," a woman faces the truth. When X-rays show irreparable damage to the spine, the athlete faces the truth. When the drunk driver stands over the coffin of his victim, he faces the truth.

Facing the truth changes priorities. Suddenly the new sofa you dreamed about purchasing is no longer important. The Caribbean trip you'd planned loses its glamour. And the ongoing battle with your spouse over who gets to drive the new car and who gets stuck driving the old one fades into insignificance.

I have always pictured this scene with Mary being thrown at Jesus' feet. I'd imagined her cowering in the dirt, hiding her face. But Scripture doesn't actually say that. The biblical writers describe her as standing "face to face" with Jesus. She had no way to avoid His gaze. She couldn't hide her shame from Him—or her guilt.

How do we look directly into the face of the pure and holy Jesus? Stripped of excuses. Stripped of society's varnish. Our entire lives laid bare before His penetrating gaze. Our futures snatched from our hands and thrust into His.

In a few short days, Jesus Himself would stand before Pontius Pilate, who seemingly held the Saviour's life in his hands. And ironically, the ruler would ask, "What is truth?" The Messiah did not answer the pontiff's question. He couldn't. For Jesus Christ doesn't merely hold truth in His hands—He is Truth. He doesn't simply possess mercy—He is Mercy. He doesn't only give life—He is Life. He doesn't just show love—He is love.

However, as Mary stood quivering before Him that morning, she didn't yet know Who it was she faced. She looked at Him as her judge and executioner, not as her Saviour. In a silence thick with anxiety, she waited for His condemnation.

"Teacher, this woman was caught red-handed in the act of adultery. Moses, in the Law, gives orders to stone such persons. What do you say?" Her accuser's words hung in the air like waterlogged long johns.

"What do you say?" That was the hook, the snare of the fowler. The temple tribunal had Him just where they wanted Him. Would He bite? How could He not respond, under the circumstances?

What would Jesus do? The traps Jesus' followers confront today haven't changed over the years. Different clothing perhaps, but the same snares, and like with Jesus, they lurk within the church's courtyard. Have you ever been tricked into playing "Pin the Tail on the Heretic?" Or "Mary Martyr?" Or "Have you heard about . . . ?" Pretended reverence for the law acts as a cloak to hide the truth. And before we know it, we find ourselves wallowing in the same filth as the accusers.

What would Jesus do? Everyone present knew what the Law of Moses decreed. They knew what part of the Judaic law the chief priests ignored and overlooked. They also knew the law of the Romans forbade anyone to take a life, even the life of a prostitute.

However, law or no law, this was the moment of truth. Those who'd been foraging for stones froze. The disciples stirred nervously, shooting warning glances at their Friend. The people in the crowd whispered and glanced over their shoulders at the self-satisfied Pharisees. The Pharisees, scribes, and temple guards folded their hands and waited to hear His reply. They waited for Him to trip, to stumble, to fumble the ball. And Mary held her breath.

Jesus paused. That's right; He paused. He took in the entire scene before taking action. He saw the hard-faced dignitaries, devoid of human pity. He read the hearts of everyone present. He gazed at the trembling woman, brought face to face with her sin.

At every encounter, at every turn, the Saviour faced the reality of sin, coiled and ready to strike. In the desert, in the leper, in the demoniac, in Jairus's dead daughter. In just a short time, He would face sin personified. He would hang on a cross.

Naked.

Friendless.

Alone.

The mob would shout insults and curses. They would laugh at His pain. They would fire their armor-piercing bullets of abuse and ridicule. And He would suffer the derision—but not because He would hang helpless or because His situation would be hopeless. Not because He would be defenseless—ten thousand angels would await for orders to fly to His rescue.

For the sake of His people, He would face the wretchedness of sin. For the sake of the woman quaking before Him, for the abusive throng, for the Pharisees plotting His demise.

Can't you hear His disciples? "Don't blow it, Jesus. Don't let Your emotions rule Your head. If ever there's a time to be politically correct, it's now!"

To be politically correct has always been fashionable, regardless of the time in history. Right, left, conservative, or liberal, as political winds shift, so blows political correctness. Last year, I could safely "save the whales;" this year, I would be politically correct to balance the budget. Peaceniks are out; "patriots" are in. Currently, it is "pc" to speak of deinstitutionalizing the government and institutionalizing the fatherless.

Old Testament Abraham was being politically correct when he told Pharaoh that Sarah was his sister, conveniently forgetting to mention that she was also his wife. During the early Christian era, several "politically correct" Christians resided in Nero's palace. The martyr Jerome renounced his faith to remain "politically correct" and alive. Later, he revealed his true colors and died for what he believed.

England's prime minister, Sir Thomas More, chose not to be politically correct when King Henry the Eighth declared himself the head of the Church of England and annulled his marriage to Catherine of Aragon so he could wed Anne Bolyn. When it came to affirming the king's

action, Sir Thomas's peers chose to be politically correct. Sir Thomas refused and lost his office, later his
head.

Perhaps the term "politically correct" should be "politically expedient?" Either way, as Jesus stood before
the restless crowd that awaited His answer, neither route
was an option to the Saviour. For Jesus to be politically
correct would doom Mary to death by stoning. To be
politically expedient would leave one precious soul to
die in her sins.

Yet, to be incorrect would cause a riot, with Mary
possibly being killed in the stampede and the Messiah's
work brought to an end before its time.

Mary stands to face her destiny, holding no hope in
her heart. Little does she know she actually stands face
to face with forgiveness.

# MARY'S TIME

*"There is a time for everything . . . under heaven . . .*
*He made everything beautiful in its time"*
(Ecclesiastes 3:1, 11, NIV).

Timing, with Jesus, is everything. This was Mary's time—not the disciples', not the temple priests', not the crowd's. Their needs would be left for another day.

Not the Pharisees' either. They, too, would face their guilt in time. The evil one had schemed to destroy the Master. Instead, Jesus used this despicable travesty of justice to bring Mary to this crucial point in her life, to the point of wanting forgiveness.

Have you ever prayed for something and wondered why God didn't answer your request immediately? You and I are creatures of immediacy. We want what we want, and we want it now! If I need money, I need it now, not after the bill becomes delinquent, not after the debt goes to the credit bureau—now! If I am sick, I want healing right away before the surgeon wields his scalpel, not after ten weeks of chemotherapy. If I am lost, I want directions instantly. I don't want to wander forty years in the wilderness before finding my way home.

God makes promises to His children. "Because you are my children, I will . . ." He repeats again and again. Scholars disagree as to how many promises the Bible contains. Their number ranges from eight thousand to thirty thousand, according to whom you ask. 2 Corinthians 1:20 says that God's promises are all Yes in Christ Jesus. God is eager to say Yes, to grant His kids the desires of their hearts (see Psalm 37:4).

The only place I ever disagree with God is in His timing. And then, only because I can't "see" the whole picture as He can. His perspective is so much broader.

However, there are two prayers we can pray that God promises to answer immediately. Immediately! No hesitation. One is the prayer of forgiveness. 1 John 1:9 promises, "If we confess our sins, He is faithful and just to forgive us our sins and to cleanse us from all unrighteousness" (KJV). Immediate! No conditions! Signed, sealed, and delivered at the cross of Jesus Christ.

The second prayer we pray that contains an instant delivery is the one Jesus made before His death. In John 16:7, Jesus promises to send His children a Comforter. No conditions. No hesitation. He lives by His Word.

The other 29,998 promises He made will be fulfilled with a resounding Yes—in His time and to the glory of His name. Those are the conditions.

Since you and I were created to praise God (see 1 Peter 2:10), we, as His royal children and heirs of His kingdom, wouldn't want the solutions to our problems to be any other way nor on any other time schedule but His.

Jesus made Himself subject to the perfect will of the Father, hence to the Father's timing. His life might be the concern of His disciples, but it wasn't His. Regardless of the mob's frenzy, the priestly fury, or the disciples' growing stress, the Son of the Living God rested securely in His Father's perfect timing. So did Mary, although she did not yet know it.

His thoughts turned to the woman cringing before Him. I can imagine a gentle smile crossing His face as He gazed at her and could see what no one else saw. Where others saw a filthy prostitute, He saw a royal heir held hostage by the father of lies. While others perceived Mary to be a boil on society's armpit, He saw a lovely daughter of eternal destiny. When others spat anger and abuse at a sniveling slut, He saw a regal princess waiting to be set free.

What a beautiful Saviour! If He could look at Mary, the whore, and see Mary, the princess, He can look at me without seeing my history of lies, of cheating, of surliness, and of pride. Instead of identifying me as Kay the liar or Kay the whiner or Kay the sarcastic (Like the Energizer‡ bunny, my list goes on and on and on . . .), He sees a daughter of the King of the universe.

Without a word, the Master Teacher knelt in the sand. I can hear the disciples whispering, "Leave it to the Master to do the unexpected." He knelt at the woman's feet. Every eye watched as the pure and holy Jesus knelt at the feet of a hooker! Incredible! The symbolism of the act that would follow in a short time would be incredible as well. Jesus would stoop low before all sin in order to release His children from their sins.

Without a word, Jesus knelt and smoothed a slate of dust. Impatient with the delay, the accusers pushed and shoved to see what the Teacher could be writing. The timid gave way to the arrogant. Jesus knew they would. He understood the curiosity He'd placed in these creatures, made in His image. He also understood the self-centered hearts of the temple authorities. He began to write in the sand.

"What is your answer, Rabbi?"

"Come on, tell us? What should we do with the slut?"

"What are you doing?"

"What *is* He doing?"

They pressed forward, badgering Him for an answer. He continued to write. Without a word, He stood to His feet and stared past the masks of righteousness into the souls of the woman's accusers. Finally, He spoke. "Whichever of you is sinless, go first: You throw the first stone."

Jesus had fulfilled the law through Moses without infringing on the authority of Rome by condemning her to death. The robes of pretended holiness were about to be torn from the would-be guardians of the law. They followed Jesus' gaze to the words He'd written in the sand.

Suddenly, their expressions changed. Their own sins lay as exposed to the world as was Mary—exposed in the presence of true Purity. Without looking up, one by one, they stole away, leaving their victim with the only one qualified to accuse her.

Unaware of what Jesus had written, Mary braced herself for the worst. After a moment of silence, she heard the shuffling of feet and a murmur of barely audible voices. She squeezed her eyes shut and held her breath, certain that at any moment she would feel the blow from a rock hitting the side of her head or the middle of her back.

But instead of feeling a striking blow, she heard a series of thuds as rocks, one after another, dropped to the ground. Her mind scrambled to make sense of what was happening. She dared not open her eyes.

The Teacher straightened and asked, "Woman?" Cautiously, Mary lifted her head. Brushing her hair back from her face, she stared about in surprise. She and the Master stood alone. Everyone was gone the priests, the Pharisees, the women, the children. Everyone. Only abandoned stones marked their memory in the temple dust. Miraculously, she had cheated death. But what price would she be required to pay to her rescuer?

Knowing that her life now belonged to this Man, she turned to Him, certain that He would expect a life of servitude and service in exchange. Lifting her eyes, she was more confused and amazed than ever. She looked not into the eyes of lust or evil, not into an expression of disdain or reproval.

Mary looked into the face of forgiveness.

"Where are they? Does no one condemn you?"

Unable to believe her good fortune, Mary whispered, "No one, Master."

"Neither do I," Jesus said.

Whatever scenarios Mary might have fantasized for escaping her doom, she could not have imagined this one. How could this be? She'd done nothing to deserve His mercy. She hadn't even asked for it. But this Man had read her heart and answered the prayer that had been repeated there for all those years.

Mary wasn't too sure how it happened, but she was grateful. Yet, the words that followed shocked her more. He simply said, "Go, and don't do it again."

Don't do it again. Don't do it again? If I had been present that day, I would have taken offense at the Master's command, "Don't do it again."

# Mary's Time

We're talking adultery here. We're talking about a common streetwalker, a tramp, a slut, a harlot, a woman of the night, a husband stealer, a home wrecker, a woman with the personal hygiene of a used Kleenex tissue!

Please understand. I am a good church lady, the daughter and grand-daughter of proper church ladies, the wife of an elder, a member of the choir, a leader of youth. Unlike this trollop, I've never strayed from the precepts and principles of the law. I have always behaved myself. I make it a point to call sin by its right name. I see the vile face of evil clearly through my corrective lenses. I am quite able to judge and reprimand when and where needed.

Tsk! To tell this woman to go and not do it again is unbelievable. Certainly, He could have advised her to clean up her act and cover her nakedness. He could have given her a lecture on the dangers of practicing unsafe sex. He could have suggested that she take classes on etiquette and proper behavior. At the very least, He should have told her to wash her face and comb her hair and to act like a lady.

If I fhad seen her being dragged into the circle, I would have wondered what the elders could be thinking, bringing such a creature into the presence of good religious women like me, and my tender-aged children. Imagine! Destroying marriages for a living!

I would have looked at her and thought, "Garbage! She's guilty as charged. Where's a rock?" But then the Master wrote in the sand. From the highest of priests and Pharisees to the lowest riffraff in the crowd, He revealed personal sins, even my sins. Embarrassed, I would have crept away, far enough to hide my shame but not so far as to miss His words "Go and don't do it again." I wouldn't have understood.

"Go and don't do it again." Christ's command to the cocaine addict,

> to the drunk,
> to the philanderer,
> to the wife beater,
> to the serial killer,
> to the child molester.

I confess, I can't understand. Forgiving is one thing. If God says He'll forgive our sins, then, I suppose, He needs to keep His word. But to add, "Go and don't do it again?" Being all too human, I can't help but think there should be some act of penance, a penal retribution, or a hair shirt to wear. Someone should be punished for the horrendous atrocities these miscreants committed.

And Someone would. In just a short time, the reparation for sin would be atoned. When Jesus forgave Mary and sent her on her way, He demonstrated the sacrifice of the cross. But no one understood.

Mary couldn't understand. I can almost see her pause and stare into Christ's compassion-filled eyes. As the truth of the Saviour's forgiveness flooded through her, she fell at His feet and worshiped Him. She worshiped Him for:

> Undeserved forgiveness.
> Unwarranted pardon.
> Unconditional love.

The past was past. The future was hers. "Go, and don't do it again!" Two thousand years later, I still find His compassion difficult to comprehend. But one look into His face of forgiveness tells me that it is real. And it is mine.

# CHAPTER FIVE

# A GENTLE UNDERSTANDING

" *'Now what do you say?'* "
(John 8:5, NIV).

We'd heard the rumors. And one glimpse of the blond sixteen-year-old Sarah assured us that the tales had been true. The girl was too pretty to be innocent. Sarah became the "topic of the day" as the students sipped their sodas at the soda shop, showered after P.E., and attended "platter" parties. We never considered including Sarah in our activities. We never talked to her; we only talked about her.

Good girls shunned Sarah. The girls with shady reputations themselves eyed her critically as well. The boys propositioned her. Teachers studied her from a distance, waiting for her to mess up again—or so it seemed to Sarah. No one peered beyond the rumors to discover the real Sarah.

Sarah had hoped to live down her reputation, but no one would let her. In their minds, she was what she was and would forever be. Once a bad apple, always a bad apple. Where there's smoke, there's fire. If a skunk looks like a skunk, acts like a skunk, and smells like a skunk, it is a skunk.

Oh yes, I remember Sarah—not for her beautiful singing voice or the "As" she received in chemistry or for her sense of humor (if she had one)—but for her reputation. I remember the girl for the rumors I'd heard about her, and yes, passed on to others.

Like a Velcro fastener, a rumor sticks. The popularity of politicians rise and fall on reputation and rumor. One bad rap—truth or fiction—can seriously affect the most revered Christian performer or preacher.

A few years back, the story circulated about a renowned Christian performer and songwriter being arrested for cocaine possession. When the truth came out, the substance found on the floor of his car was 100 percent enriched wheat flour. But somehow the truth wasn't as "naughty" as the lie, and the fallacious rumor stuck. Each of us can name preachers and performers who "lost their way," or so it was reported along the evangelical "rumor net." The good they did faded in the glare of their "sins."

That was before words like Internet, Information super highway, and Web page had been invented. Today, a tidbit of gossip about a fellow believer or a rank rumor regarding a less-than-righteous brother can circle the globe before nightfall. "How to Become a Spiritual Pariah in Fifteen Seconds or Less." What a title for a magazine article on gossip and the World Web!

Reputation and Rumor. The boy Jesus understood the meaning of these words. He grew up under the unremitting eye of public censure. Rumors swirled around

Him. Born under questionable circumstances, His mother acquired a bad reputation. Don't think the good ladies of Nazareth couldn't count back nine months from the little boy's birthday. According to their mathematics, Mary became pregnant with Jesus out of wedlock.

Whenever the ladies of the community gathered at the well to draw the family's daily water supply and to gossip, they lifted knowing eyebrows and grew silent whenever Mary joined their group. The young Jesus saw the ribald grins the local men directed toward Mary. The Son felt the pain that coursed His lovely mother's face as a result. It pierced His heart as well.

Some biblical scholars suggest that this unremitting censure directed toward His mother must have contributed to the reason Jesus Christ dealt so gently with fallen women. Firsthand, He recognized how cruel society could be toward women with questionable pasts. He had seen their hurt and embarrassment in His own mother's eyes.

When correcting men, His words were, at times, severe. But whenever the Saviour dealt with a woman of questionable character, He spoke with tenderness and compassion. Second, when He looked into the eyes of a fallen woman, He knew the circumstances that led the woman into her sin. And He felt His mother's pain once again.

And third, He understood the general condition of women's role, the society of His day. He'd come to planet Earth to minister to these very ones—those who were oppressed, those hanging on the very margins of society, those trodden underfoot like so much garbage. Other than the victims of leprosy, no group of people better fit this profile than did the women of His day.

In ancient Judaism, a female presence was often evident and respected as is clearly seen in the records of Miriam, Delilah, Jezebel, Rebecca, Anna, Sarah, and Ruth. Some believe that many of the social restrictions for women came when people shifted from pastoral living to city life.

The need for more security, as the city dwellers came in contact with people outside the clan, set the stage for a more restrictive existence for women. Decent women seldom appeared in public. When they did, they wore a heavy veil.

A woman's only release from the confines of her home came when she drew water from the town well several times a day. This made the well the social center of the Jewish world. Women came to the well for water and to socialize with other women.

The exceptions to these restrictions were the yearly feasts such as Passover, Pentecost, and Tabernacles, which were celebrated in Jerusalem. On such occasions, the young bucks of the community got to "eye" the latest crop of eligible spouse material.

A woman's relationship to a man defined her value in society. Before marriage, she belonged to her father, whom she addressed as master or lord. To him, she owed absolute obedience. Like her mother, she was part of the household belonging to the father. In the Decalogue, the wife is listed with other possessions: male and female slave, ox, donkey.

A daughter could own no property. She had no rights of inheritance unless she had no brothers. She could make no vows or contracts without her father's approval.

Any earnings she made belonged to her father. Her witness could not be accepted in court. If she were raped, the father would take her case to court and also receive payment of fifty shekels of silver for the damage done to the father's goods. The rapist would be forced to marry the girl and not allowed to ever divorce her.

Joseph Grass, in his book *Mary Magdelene and the Women in Jesus' Life,* notes that if an engaged girl was raped within the town limits, she was stoned to death along with the man, because she should have cried for help. (See Deuteronomy 22:23-27.) If the rape occurred in open country, only the man would be stoned. The reason given for this judgment is, "He dishonored the future wife of a neighbor." The injured party was the man, not the girl herself (Kansas City, Mo.: Shied and Ward, 1980) 66.

A daughter was her father's to treasure or to sell into slavery should he so desire. Upon marriage, at an age less than twelve years old, the young girl transferred her obeisance from her father to her new master, her husband.

Any woman not under the protection of a male family member was "open season" to unscrupulous men. A woman divorced by her husband, was given a written document, countersigned by two witnesses, that said, "You are free to every man" (The opposite, a man divorced by his wife, did not exist) (ibid. 67).

If abandoned by her husband, a woman's children stayed with the father. The ex-wife became a nonperson in society, an outcast. Earning a living was impossible, since women did not work outside the home. The divorced woman had limited ways to support herself beyond that of prostitution. Some Bible scholars suggest that Rahab of the Old Testament was one such example. Perhaps that was their way of sanitizing the story.

The disciples "marveled" at the attention Jesus gave to women—especially those women of ill-repute. The Greek word *thaumazo*, used here, means to "strongly wonder." We might say, "I really wonder about Him." It could mean to question His sanity. They were horrified to have the Master converse with such individuals. It just wasn't done in refined society.

When the disciples returned to the well from the Samaritan town to find Christ speaking with the woman of questionable morals, they were indignant. With all the fury He caused in the vicinity of Jerusalem, couldn't He at least refrain from breaking the social rules while in Samaria?

In speaking to the woman at the well, Jesus broke at least three social rules by which the Jewish society lived.

First, she was a woman. Men didn't speak with women in public, even their own wives. The moral code of the Hebrew fathers decreed, "Do not have much speech with women; and if this applies to your own wife, so much the more to wives of others . . . Anyone who speaks much with women does himself harm, because, turning away from his studies, he ends up acquiring hell" (ibid. 65).

A wife's place was to ease her husband's life so that he could dedicate more time to his religious studies. She had no purpose to study on her own, of course, since he would interpret the law for her, as much as it would apply to a mere woman.

A Jewish rabbi, or teacher, would never consider instructing a woman. To show how Jesus broke this code of conduct, Martha later announced to Mary, "The Teacher is asking for you." He was her Teacher. Each time He included women in His discourse, He tweaked the noses of the Jewish hierarchy, including those of His own disciples. The women who followed Him and His disciples flaunted the rules of their time (see Luke 8:1-3, 23:49, 24:6-10).

Second, she was a stranger and a foreigner. No proper Jew would consider speaking to a person from her unclean heritage. It would take several generations of "Jewishness" before her lineage could be cleansed of these impurities.

Third, she was a fallen woman. Someone passing by might think He was propositioning her, or she, Him. Just the fact that she spoke to Him at all labeled her as a trollop. A good woman would never consider speaking to a strange man. Imagine the questions that went through this woman's mind regarding the Stranger. What a struggle she must have had deciding whether or not to reply. The smart move for her would have been to ignore Him and to scurry home with or without the water.

From the disciples' perspective, Jesus had broken too many such laws already. Surely, such social intercourse could only bring additional censure to the kingdom of God and the cause of the Messiah.

How many times have I chosen to do the expedient thing or the socially safe thing when the Holy Spirit was urging me to break the taboos, forget my inhibitions, dare to reach out beyond society's barriers.

A young woman sat on a bench sipping a Coke™ in

the middle of the local mall. She wore a soiled tee shirt with the message "NO FEAR" emblazoned across her back and a pair of faded blue jeans. With her head bent forward, her long stringy hair hid her features. But from the heaving of the shoulder, any passerby who gave her more than a glance could tell she was crying.

I paused at the window of a shop, ostensibly studying the items in the wind, but watching her. I felt drawn to this desperate stranger. A Voice within me said, "Go to her. Put your arm around her. She needs someone."

My innards shook like gelatin. "No, Lord, I can't walk up to a stranger and . . . what will she think?"

"Go to her," the Voice, something I could feel rather than hear, insisted. I exhaled sharply. "With all the weirdos around, she'll think . . ."

"Go to her."

"What if she wants more than I can give? Richard would die if I came home with a . . . I can't even afford to offer her a hot meal . . ." My list of objections continued. I walked past her and studied another store window. I turned away and struggled with myself for several seconds. When I finally turned around and started back toward her, she was gone.

The young woman haunted my thinking for weeks, perhaps even months. Even today, a couple years later, I remember her with regret. Not only did I fail to comfort one of Jesus' precious daughters, I missed the blessing He planned for me to receive.

But the Master recognized the person and her need, not her gender. And He did not fail to act. And with His action, He placed the ethics of responsibility and love above the ethics of the law. His example and His words teach us to regard women as daughters of God, broadcasters of the Good News, who, together with men, are invited to join the family of God. First Peter 3:7 uses the expression of equality "*sugkleronomois*," or "coheirs," a term used in state law at that time.

At the well, Jesus could no more have passed by the woman, He could no more have shunned her or ignored her, than the Good Shepherd could keep from rescuing a lamb that had fallen into a ravine—societies niceties or not. To do so would have denied who He was. This the disciples could not understand.

That the woman became one of His disciples, that she brought the gospel to her community, is extremely unusual. One of the first breakthroughs to the non-Jewish group came about through the conversion of many Samaritans. It was a direct result of this encounter with Jesus.

Perhaps it took a woman living on the outer rim of society to carry the gospel into the community, since a proper lady would not have the latitude necessary to travel beyond the confines of her own home. She took the initiative of faith. And we don't even know her name.

Jewish society believed that each woman's fulfillment was in a man. Jesus came to show that each woman's fulfillment is in God. God gives them the right and the power to become something beyond themselves. God gives you and me that right as well.

# FACE TO FACE WITH FORGIVENESS

# *Section*
# 2

# Mary, the Disciple

# CHAPTER SIX

# SITTING AT HIS FEET

*"She had a sister called Mary,
who sat at the Lord's feet"*
(Luke 10:39).

I admire a woman who naturally possesses the talent of hospitality. You know the one I mean. She opens her spotless home to guests on a minute's notice. Her perfectly appointed table puts Martha Stewart and Laura Ashley to shame. She is positively unflappable, regardless of the number of guests she must serve. A pot of pasta or a bowl of Boston baked beans makes little difference. Served by this talented woman, the simplest of food becomes a banquet.

Over the years, preachers and scholars have likened the "hostess with the mostess" to Martha of Bethany. As a woman and a less-than-perfect hostess, I believe Martha was not one of these gifted gals. By the sound of it, she was more like me. She liked having guests, especially the Teacher of Nazareth and His entourage. But any hostess can tell you that entertaining guests and enjoying guests can be two distinctly different experiences.

# FACE TO FACE WITH FORGIVENESS

I enjoy having guests in my home. It's the before and after that throws me. Before they arrive, I worry that all will go well. And after they leave, I worry that perhaps all didn't go as well as I'd hoped.

I joke about asking my husband how tall the male guests are so that I can know whether or not I need to clean the top of my refrigerator before they arrive. But a part of me is deadly serious. It's a fragment of my "perfection mode," my desire to look perfect in everyone's eyes. Notice the "look perfect?" Looking perfect has nothing to do with being perfect.

I like to think that Martha suffered from the same perfection problem. Considering that she couldn't pop a little casserole into her microwave on short notice and that preparing a meal took most of the day, feeding in excess of twenty people was much more a chore for her than for me.

I imagine she had a servant or two to pare the potatoes. And the other women in Jesus' entourage must have rolled up their collective sleeves to knead the bread. Yet, with such a major cook-a-thon, an extra pair of hands, regardless of how inept they might be around culinary confines, would be helpful, especially when those hands happen to belong to a wayward sister.

Over the years, I can hear Martha rag on her younger sister about Mary's decidedly unladylike behavior. Then, after Mary's "fall". . . Hmmm . . . The shame the girl managed to bring upon the family would have disturbed many nights of sleep for the hovering older sister.

How thrilled Martha must have been when the Teacher forgave her little sister's sins and granted her life, not once but seven times! Martha must have thought, *Here's Mary's opportunity to prove her refor-mation from a woman of the gutter to a woman of grace. So, what is she doing sitting in the parlor with the men? Will the girl never learn?*

I wonder if Martha felt a little like the older brother in the story of the prodigal son. Had she, the family's "good girl," found herself returning to the shadows following Mary's conversion?

In the story of the prodigal son, the older brother complained that he'd spent his entire life being the good son and the father never fixed prime rib for him and his friends. What about all those nights he'd set up with ailing cattle? All the days bending his back in the hot sun bringing in the harvest? All those years mucking out the stalls? Was there a Thank you, a word of appre-ciation, recognition for faithful service?

But here his father was throwing a party because his little brother had squandered his father's fortune and returned home penniless and filthy, with his tail be-tween his legs! Is it any wonder the older brother re-sented the hullabaloo surrounding his brother's return?

Surely, Martha must have had similar thoughts. Martha had always been the obedient, conscientious daughter, the one who ran to retrieve her papa's slip-pers and who continued to keep the family together years after the parents left the scene. Good old faithful Martha, cleaning up the messes Mary always seemed to make. But about as interesting as an old shoe compared to her flashy and naughty younger sister.

Like the prodigal son, Mary always seemed to be mess-ing up her life and the lives of those around her. And there she was, sitting at Jesus' feet, basking in His favor, while good old Martha slaved in the kitchen. Even the most saintly of women would harbor a scrap of resentment.

Yet, Martha wasn't completely without recognition. Having the popular Teacher as a guest at her table must have been a coup over the other women of Galilee. The Preacher had performed extensive miracles in the area. He was a "most eligible bachelor." This must have pleased the elder sister, a pleasant contrast with the reputation Mary had acquired over the years. All would have been perfect except for one little irritation—Mary.

If I'd been Martha, I would have sputtered as I popped the beans, muttered as I mashed the potatoes, and whined as I whipped the butter. The atmosphere in the kitchen would have been purple with resentment and green with envy. I would cringe when a round of laughter reached my burning ears or the sound of the Master's voice rose and fell with melodious truths. Yet, I would have paused in the parlor doorway several times before I actually voiced my grievance.

And secretly, down deep inside of me would have been a "piece" of Mary—a young girl wishing she, too, could escape, wishing she, too, could toss aside her inhibitions, wishing she, too, could forsake her rigid code of behavior and join in the fun, just once.

But no, Martha was the proper daughter, the one who never broke the rules, never leaned toward the whimsy, never chased butterflies in the field or examined a caterpillar in her fingers. Martha knew that someone had to maintain the household, someone had to pay the bill collectors, someone had to prepare and serve the daily bread. And she had no doubt who that someone would always be.

But wait, I can't know what Martha thought that day as she assembled her favorite recipe for Jericho lamb stew. I wasn't there. As a woman, I can only suppose. Her thoughts could have been nobler than mine. She could have feared for her sister's reputation. She could have been protecting her foolish younger sibling.

Mary's track record with men had never been noteworthy. And here Mary was, breaking society's rules once again, surrounded by men. Martha had seen her sister reform and fail several times. Had not the Master Himself forgiven Mary seven times? The perfect number—seven.

Martha had observed the changes in Mary's countenance. Peace had replaced the looks of sadness in her sister's countenance. And Martha had hoped, and prayed, and held her breath. Wariness could have prompted Martha's behavior.

Whatever thoughts she might have had, help with food preparation was more of an excuse than a reason. Chances are, Martha was like most of us, a jumble of emotions, some altruistic, some selfish, some even she couldn't understand. Yet, Someone did understand.

Jesus knew and understood Martha's distractions that day. From where He sat, talking with His beloved disciples, He could read Martha's motives as she prepared the dinner meal in the next room. The Saviour's heart must have yearned to deliver Martha from the rigid code that restrained her from joining Him in the parlor.

It wasn't her body that needed setting free. She wasn't physically chained to the kitchen. Iron bars didn't separate her from the Master. The chains of protocol were forged on her heart, ironclad manacles of opinion and habit restricted her mind.

You know what I mean. We all wear them. Cultural inhibitions, forged through the generations, often keep us from opening our minds and truly listening to the Saviour's words.

Simple things can sometimes hold us in check. Take this example: For years, I refused to use sponges to clean my kitchen counters because I remembered my mother saying they were unsanitary. Not that a sponge could be more unsanitary than a dirty dish rag! It wasn't until I was in my forties that I realized sponges or dish rags both held the same disease germs if one doesn't change them regularly.

Duh! Bright, huh? It took me so long to discover that nugget of truth?

If I can become so hung up on such a small thing as a kitchen sponge, imagine what cultural laws I faithfully observe as spiritual truth! If I never take the time to search for God's truth buried within, I will never know the freedom of which Jesus spoke in John 8:32, "Ye shall know the truth, and the truth shall make you free" (KJV).

There was nothing wrong with Martha expecting her sister to be in the kitchen with the women. Even today, the woman who lingers too long within a circle of men is subject to censure. I know that for me there have been times I longed to be in the parlor listening to the men discuss some exciting political or spiritual situation rather than in the kitchen listening to the newest mother of the group talk about her difficult delivery or about her child's diaper rash.

I admire a hostess who can steer the conversation

around mentally challenging topics while stirring her simmering pot of gravy at the same time. What a legacy she would pass on to her daughters and to her younger sisters-in-Christ.

When I chatted with my older sister, Connie, about Martha, Connie asked, "But, what if Martha had abandoned the kitchen and sat down beside her sister to listen? Then what? When dinner time came, how happy would her guests have been?"

I thought about Connie's question for some time. It would have been interesting to see how the Lord would have handled the problem. Would He have shocked the sandals off His disciples by suggesting "they" retire to the kitchen to help with the food preparation? Or would He have multiplied Martha's day-old bread and left-over fish chowder to feed the hungry household? Of course, He could always stir up a batch of manna as a last resort. What miracle would Martha and her guests have enjoyed if she'd chosen the better part as did her sister, Mary? I guess we'll never know.

Instead of incredible miracles filling Martha's senses, unnecessary distractions kept her mind from receiving the truths He preached. The distractions were more of a burden than were the physical tasks to be done.

Recently, I was helping clean up after a potluck in an unfamiliar church kitchen (somewhere in the Continental United States). As I stacked the soiled serving dishes beside a sink to be washed, I spied a detailed, typewritten, plastic-encased instruction sheet on the accepted technique of washing dishes in that sink. Yes, that's right. Someone took the time to write out dishwashing instructions for her sisters, down to how many squirts of liquid dish detergent to add to the water for optimum cleansing.

I laughed. Whoever this exacting sister might be, I bet she was a bundle to handle in her church family. Then I remembered that every church family has one or more of them—what the world calls a "bean counter." Always precise. Ever exacting. Incredibly correct.

No one could fault the dear woman who had carefully mounted the dish-washing instructions. When you're right, you're right. Right? The problem comes when being right spills over on others, when Miss Right insists that everyone else be right as well. In time, Miss Right may find herself left to be and do the right thing her way. Right—but totally alone.

Before you get the idea I'm against people who organize their time and who insist on doing the best job possible and in the right manner, many of the people I love (especially in my extended family) are bean counters and list makers. I depend on them to organize me, take charge of all details that are too much of a bother for me.

Every church needs 'em. If a church only has Marys who sit and adore the truth or Lazaruses who share their stories, they'll be in trouble when the first fuse blows or the PA system begins picking up a radio talk show. But Martha, dear Martha, filled her brain with worries and her heart with resentment.

As Jesus talked, I can imagine Him silently coaxing Martha to open up, to admit to her feelings. He knew that only as she recognized her problem could He help her. As long as she stayed sequestered in her kitchen, she could not receive His healing power.

Like malignant tumors, envy, resentment, and worry fester within until recognized and treated by the Great Physician. For whatever motive, Martha finally admitted she had a problem. She interrupted the Master's discourse.

What was Jesus saying when Martha broke into the conversation? Was He relating the glories of the kingdom of God, the joy found in truly loving one another, His adventure with the "deviled ham?" Imagine, interrupting the Saviour! Such an action is almost unthinkable to me.

Or is it? How many times have I interrupted the Saviour's message with trivia like, "Why in the world did Andrea buy a dress like that? It's definitely not her color!" or "Looks like Cindy is about to deliver. We'd better hold her baby shower soon. I wonder how next Tuesday evening would be for everyone?" or "Oh No! Who set that vase of flowers on the organ? The water could ruin the finish!"

Interrupting the Saviour's message with trivia. I do it all the time. During a church service, my mind wanders. I see a bee buzzing above an elder's head or detect a spot on the new carpet,or notice a songbook about to slide off the piano bench. My spiritual mind gives way to my physical mind, and the Saviour's message is interrupted. I find myself standing in the doorway with Martha instead of sitting at the feet of Jesus with Mary.

Who knows what spiritual gem, what word of encouragement, or what nugget of joy could have been mine?

# CHAPTER SEVEN

# MARTHA INTERRUPTED

*Martha interrupted, saying, " 'Master, don't you care that my sister has abandoned the kitchen to me? Tell her to lend me a hand?' "*
(Luke 10:40, *The Message*).

Oops! Martha revealed much more about herself than she'd intended in her remarks. She probably spoke the very thoughts the disciples had in their minds as well. What was Mary, a woman, doing sitting with the men? Men gather to discuss ideas; women gather to discuss food preparation. Men develop the great philosophies of life; women serve the men.

Society demanded that Martha serve Christ, not because He was her Guest, but because she was a woman. You can be certain that the tax collectors, Zacchaeus and Matthew, didn't rush to the kitchen to prepare food when Jesus visited their homes. No, they assigned either servants or women to take care of that detail while they sat at the feet of Jesus absorbing the truths falling from His lips.

Jesus believed in women's liberation. He came to set

all His people free, including the female gender. He didn't come to revolutionize the laws of the land or the social structure of Judea. He came to liberate the hearts of His people, not their bodies.

Does that mean Jesus didn't recognize the necessity for Martha to feed her guests? I don't think so. Matthew reported that Jesus said, " 'Don't worry about what you will eat and what you will drink' " (Matthew 6:31, author's paraphrase). This was the message the Saviour wanted Martha to receive. Martha needed to eat of the food He had prepared instead of the other way around.

Another view of Jesus and food service was when He fed the five thousand. This stunned the disciples—not only the miracle, but the act. When Christ fed the multitude, He assumed the female role in society by "preparing" the food for the crowd. Then, to add to the disciples' consternation, He asked them to serve the food, also women's work. It wasn't as if there weren't adequate numbers of women present who could have assumed the task, but He gave them the assignment.

Repeatedly, the Saviour demonstrated His views on society's restrictions for women by performing the tasks assigned to them. When Jesus took the children on His lap and said, "Unless you become like this child, you'll never be ready to enter God's kingdom," He rattled the cultural chains regarding children and women once again. Children were left to the care of the women. The men of Judah could not be bothered with the frivolities of the young. They had deeper, more important issues to consider and debate—issues like the coming Messiah and His kingdom.

Jesus knew that by setting Martha free from her cultural chains she would find her physical service to be a delight, not a chore. The Master was preparing the disciples as well. He needed to shock them out of society's "men's club."

By freeing the disciples of their preconceived notions, He was training them for the greater service to come after His return to the Father.

Peter, James, Paul, and the other apostles would need to understand the importance of the ministry of New Testament women. The early Christian church would function and grow due to the efforts of women like Tabitha, Lydia, Priscilla, and so many others. And later, throughout history, women like Joan of Arc, Katherine Luther, Anne Hutchinson, you, and me would fulfill our tasks for Him only if we could understand our position in the kingdom of God, not as female-servants but as beloved daughters of the King of the universe.

On that day, in the ceramic-tiled parlor in Bethany, Martha and the disciples didn't understand Jesus' intentions. They did, however, understand society's code. They all knew that Mary's behavior cast aspersions on Jesus as well. They all wondered, "Doesn't He know or care that the young woman is behaving unseemly?"

Obviously, they thought Mary hadn't shed all her questionable habits when the Saviour cleansed her of her sins. Since Luke was the only gospel writer to record this event, we can't accurately read the disciples' thinking, but later, at the feast of Simon, some of their thoughts would surface.

And Lazarus, what about Lazarus? Where was he in the story? Was his a "hands off " policy when it came to the domestic operation of his home? Was he an indulgent brother who found it difficult to reprimand his little sister? Did he always let Martha do the "dirty work"?

One thing that bothers me in this story is, Why did Martha direct her complaint to Jesus instead of to Mary? I can't imagine blaming my guest because my sister wasn't in the kitchen helping me.

"Don't You care that my sister has left me to do the work by myself?" Could she have said it partially in jest? I can't understand why she would direct her barbs at a guest in her home. Was she questioning the Master's compassion for her lot in life? If so, this I can understand.

"Don't You care, Lord, that I have a toothache? Don't you care, Lord, that I can't pay my bills this month? Don't You care that my husband is seeing another woman?"

How many times have I questioned my Saviour's concern for me? Oh, I know He forgives sins, but does He forgive mine? And I know that He heals diseases, but mine? And He directs the paths of His children, are you sure He means me?

But back to Martha. Most sisters would talk directly to their erring sibling. Why didn't she side up to Mary and whisper in her ear, "You'll get yourself out to the kitchen and help me, girl, if you know what's good for you!" To accuse the Master for her sister's apparent social faux pas? How impolite. It's almost as if Martha wanted to point out the sin of her sister as a way of enhancing her own "goodness."

Have you ever heard the faithful "saint" announcing before the congregation, "We need to be praying for . . ."

then waxing eloquent with all the juicy details of the latest scandal surrounding the erring one? Or how about the spicy yarn that begins with, "Now, I'm not one to judge, but . . ." or "Isn't it sad about . . ." Invisible wounds inflicted in the name of "goodness."

Accusations cloaked with righteousness are no less damning than those splayed across the headlines of Hollywood's trashiest tabloid. The good "church lady" who righteously reports to the pastor that she saw one of her "brothers" enter a porno house becomes aligned with the original accuser of the brethren, just as surely as the town gossip.

This is very much like Satan. Being the author of deception, his methods are so clever that only the Holy Spirit can enable us to catch him in the act. It began long ago. Satan criticized God. He implied that God was unfair then spread the innuendo throughout all heaven until other angels rebelled against God.

Man learned to criticize quickly. Adam blamed Eve. Eve blamed Satan. And so the destructive chain continues down through history.

Like radio waves transmitted through the air, Satan, the "prince of the power of the air," can bombard our minds with critical thoughts. Then he convinces us we have a certain "intuitive wisdom" about people. There's a pride in judging, of being "in the know." Judging is a heavy burden because the spirit of criticism can never be satiated.

Criticism follows a predictable pattern. First, we think negative thoughts. Second, we look for weaknesses and mistakes in others. Third, we pride ourselves in our ability to discern the evil in others. And we're trapped in the frenzied cycles to feed the cancerous habit of criticism.

Unfortunately, it doesn't stop here. The fourth step is criticizing God. We actually begin to believe it's OK to give God advice. We're sure we have a better idea than our Creator.

When the disciples came to Jesus and suggested He call down fire from heaven on the heads of some strangers healing in Jesus' name, the Lord said, "You do not know what manner of spirit you are of. For the Son of man did not come to destroy." (Luke 9:55, NKJV)

Jesus outlined the proper procedure for handling interpersonal problems between spiritual siblings. "If ye have ought against any . . ." (Mark 11:25, KJV). By going to a third person with my grievance against a brother or sister, I malign the character of the accused in another person's eyes and burden the other person with knowledge that will forever sully his view of the accused. Jesus said go directly to my brother or sister. And then only if I love him so much that I would willingly die for him.

That's strong language. How many people do you know for whom you would willingly give your life? Your spouse? Your kids? Your best friend? It certainly limits one's realm of censure, doesn't it? And then to do it in tenderness and love? Wow! Imagine the revolution that would occur in our churches if we carried out God's plan. What a revolution would occur in my life and my home if I treated those closest to me as Jesus commanded!

Going to a third party with the sins of another instead of directly to the offender draws one's own motives into question. Why would I choose to report to the pastor or the boss instead of to the offender? Fear? To merit favor, like a first-grader tattling to her teacher? Usually, when I feel the urge to "report" on a brother or sister, there is very little holiness involved but a whole lot of self-righteousness.

Before Jesus replied to her question, Martha added, "Tell her to help me!" Not only was Martha telling the Lord how to solve the "help" problem in the kitchen, but she set herself up as judge and probationer of her sister and as an accuser of the Lord of lords.

Jesus ignored the accusation. I'm glad. All I have to do is remember all the unfair accusations I've leveled at Him and I must fall on my knees in thanksgiving. I can almost hear the Master sigh. How audacious of us to judge one another when the Son of the Living God said, "I did not come to judge the world!" If He refused to judge, how can we suppose we have the right to do so? But judge Martha did.

I wonder how long she stewed in the kitchen before she spoke up? Were the other women of Jesus' entourage with Martha, egging her on with their arched eyebrows and simpering censure? How long did Martha wait, expecting Jesus to send Mary out to the kitchen to help. How many pans had she banged in fury? How many cupboard doors had she slammed trying to get His attention? Or Mary's?

Did Mary hear the pans clang and the doors slam? Or had she been so engrossed in what her Saviour was saying that she truly did not catch Martha's not-so-subtle hints? We don't know if Mary's behavior to escape Martha's work detail was habitual or out-of-the-ordinary.

But we do know that nothing could have deterred Mary from staying at Jesus' feet.

One Christmas, a second cousin of mine visited my parents' home. Instantly, I became totally enamored with the dashing soldier and his snappy uniform. Kenneth had been stationed in Germany in the years following World War II. He had seen the death camps of Auschwitz and Dachou. He told about standing guard in the prison where several of Hitler's henchmen awaited trial.

As a child of eight, I sat on Kenneth's lap while he told his gruesome stories to the adults. My mother, afraid I might have bad dreams, tried to lure me away from Kenneth. This worked for a short time, but as soon as possible, I returned for more horrid thrills. As a result, I had nightmares about concentration camps and the Gestapo long after the memory of Kenneth's visit faded.

What a contrast my fixation with my cousin was compared to Mary's adoration of Jesus. While Kenneth told stories of death, deprivation, and destruction, Jesus spoke of life, renewal, and forgiveness. Mary had spent years searching for love in all the wrong places. And once she found the genuine love of the Saviour, there was nothing in this world that could have drawn her from His side. While I fell in love with a handsome war hero, Mary fell in love with her Creator, who was also her Re-creator.

Some people would like to put sexual overtones to Mary's relationship with Christ. The musical, "Jesus Christ, Superstar," celebrates this travesty of God's love. To be certain, Mary must have had sexual thoughts regarding the Teacher at the start. That's the only way she'd ever related to men since arriving at puberty. But as she drew nearer to His side, as she listened to His Words, and as she watched Him interact with others, it became obvious to her that His love went far beyond any human sexuality she'd ever imagined. To think He could love her without any strings attached must have melted her cynical heart.

God's Word says Mary sat at His feet. How often she must have heard, "And the kingdom is likened unto . . ." What hope! What joy! The kingdom of God was within her grasp for the first time in her life. Nothing else was important to Mary that day; not food, not society's acceptance, not even her family's approval. To be close to the Master, to bask in His love, and to listen to His words; that's what mattered. There was nothing sexual about Mary's adoration. She'd been forgiven much, so she loved much. While Martha wished to *do* for the Lord, Mary only desired to gaze lovingly into God's face and be caught up in the rapture of His presence.

When Jesus sought His followers, He didn't seek obedient but dispassionate servants. His was a look for a passionate love so strong it burned all other bounds. Cold and calculated lip service has never been enough for our God. God's love for His people is so intense that our betrayal is described as adultery.

Mary understood the kind of relationship the Saviour expected and was eager to give it. David could have been writing of Mary's adoration in Psalm 63:

> Oh God, You are my God;
> Early will I seek You;
> My soul thirsts for You;

My flesh longs for You
In a dry and thirsty land
Where there is no water. . . .
Because Your lovingkindness is
better than life,
My lips shall praise You. . . .
My soul shall be satisfied as with
marrow and fatness,
And my mouth shall praise You
with joyful lips. . . .
I meditate on You in the night
watches. . . .
My soul follows close behind You (NKJV).

The Song of Songs legitimizes the deep and passionate love between a husband and wife as an illustration of the love God wants with His people. Passages like, "He brought me to His banqueting house, and His banner over me is life. Sustain me with cakes of raisins, refresh me with apples, for I am lovesick" (Song of Solomon 2:4, 5, LB Author's paraphrase).

A later passage in the story says, " when I found the one I loved, I held Him and would not let him go" (Song of Solomon 3:4, LB author's paraphrase).

Mary's love reflects what Moses wrote in Deuteronomy 6:5: "Love the Lord your God with all your heart and with all your soul and with all your strength" (NIV). For her, being a follower of Christ went beyond obedience to the ultimate issue of love. She knew that a faith of ethical dos and don'ts, apart from adoration, was not the faith Jesus represented.

Biblical scholars point out that the proper definition

of disciple means "sitting at the feet of Jesus." Mary's quiet contemplation of Jesus Christ was a segment of a circle, an intimate circle of love. God gives the desire to love Him; hence, love is returned to Him, which prompts more love from Him, causing love to be returned, and so on.

Jesus poured out His love on Mary by forgiving her and elevating her to royalty status. She adored Him in return.

For Mary, the world was a cold and lonely place, a place where she'd been used, abused and cast aside like a used Kleenex tissue. Once she'd tasted the real thing, nothing else mattered. She simply wanted to "bathe in the ocean of God's love instead of experience it drop by drop." Gary Thomas, Sacred Pathways (Nashville, Tenn.: Thomas Nelson, 1996. 217).

That day in Bethany, the infant Christian, Mary, took her first step toward genuine worship and praise.

CHAPTER EIGHT

# DAUGHTER OF WORRY

*" 'Martha, Martha, the Lord answered,*
*you are worried and upset about many things,*
*but only one thing is needed' "*
(Luke 10:41, NIV).

Sometimes I think I have a generous dollop of both sisters in my makeup. Sometimes when I see others basking in the Lord's favor, I lament over my "goodness."

Sometimes all those necessary tasks I perform for the Master become burdens of resentment instead of joyful opportunities of service.

Sometimes, in the deeper recesses of my being, I cry, "Lord, don't You see what I'm doing for You? The sacrifices I am making to serve You? I'm tired, Lord. Can't You make Cynthia or Ruthie or . . ." and I name off several of my more 'fortunate' friends, ". . . pitch in and help?"

In 1 Corinthians 3:9, Paul calls us "labourers together with God" (KJV). However, when my work for God gets in the way of my concentration on Him, I find the burden too heavy to carry, and I burn out. Like Martha, I am crushed by the load.

Oswald Chambers, in *My Utmost for His Highest*, writes, "The one concern of a worker should be concentration on God. And this will mean that all the other margins of life, mental, normal and spiritual, are free with the freedom of a child, a worshiping child, not a wayward child . . . . We are freed for one thing only—to be absolutely devoted to our co-Worker" (An updated Edition in Today's Language, James Reimann, ed. (Nashville, Tenn.: Thomas Nelson, 1992) 23.

The modern-day phenomenon of job burnout often originates with feelings of being overworked and under-appreciated. Whether real or imagined, the results are the same. Resentment takes root. Stress grows. Joy withers and dies, sapping the body of necessary strength and energy, creating a spiral of weakness and disease.

Several years ago, I went through such a burnout. In the process of grieving over the loss of my position and the loss of my self-worth, I searched for comfort from the demoralizing pain. I turned to Mrs. See's for relief and Mr. Bresler for comfort. I found temporarily relief in chocolate-covered pecan carmels and triple hot fudge sundaes. However, they only worked for so long. When my problems grew along with my dress size, I sought out Optifast™ for a new "comforter." From there I see-sawed between the two until my misery consumed me. It wasn't until I heeded my Saviour's advice and turned to the Comforter He supplied that my healing began. My healing began from the inside out, and He's still healing me.

Jesus could see that Martha was upset about many

things, things that had nothing to do with the stress of preparing a meal. His reply reached beyond the surface tension to her heart when He said, "Martha, Martha, you are upset and worried about many things."

How sad. In the kitchen, out of reach of the Son of God—or so she thought—Martha fretted and worried. All that time, her relief and the Answer to her destructive frame of mind sat but a room away. "All of our frets and worries come from calculating without God."

I am a reformed worrier. I come from a long, proud line of fretters and worriers. My mother, my grandmother, my great-grandmother could give any worrier a run for her worries. Therefore, to become a worrier was as natural for me as tipping the bottle can be for the child of an alcoholic. I could worry myself sick over the most fantastic problems, all created in my imagination.

An example, my daughter, Kelli, and son-in-law, Mark, are touring the world with the inter-denominational Christian singing group, "The Celebrant Singers." The Celebrant Singers organization sends out seven teams to various places all over the world. Kelli and Mark's tour will take them to the Far East this year. As a worrier, I would periodically worry myself to illness with horrid scenarios of evil and destruction that could—the operative word is could—that could happen to my precious children.

For those of you not addicted to worry, let me explain. Creative worrying is like spending a lonely Saturday night reading *Foxe's Book of Martyrs*, the Christian's equivalent to videos like "The House on Elm Street" or "The Omen." There's a negative adrenaline charge that flows through the worrier, bringing with it a demon of depression that casts the worrier into a hellish pit of discouragement and defeat.

But if, as a child of God, I believe God's promise in Hebrews 13:5 where it says, " 'Never will I leave you; never will I forsake you' " (NIV). I must believe that the promise is also meant for my children, who are on a mission for Him. Therefore, I cannot worry, I cannot fret, without casting aspersions on my Saviour. When I fret, I announce to the universe that I do not really believe God will keep His word. I am saying that the Creator of the universe cannot handle the problems of the world without me.

That day in Bethany, Martha believed she was bearing her worries alone. And she was, until she came to Jesus. Then it happened. Tenderly, carefully, the Saviour peeled away each layer of stress to reveal His hostess's deepest need: "only one thing is needed."

What a comfort it is to know that Jesus knows exactly what I need. He sees my "inmost being." He is ready to grant me the true desires of my heart; not the whimsical, candy store wants and desires but the deep down, inmost desires. And these desires are always answered *yes* in Christ Jesus. It wasn't until Jesus brought Martha face to face with her real desire that she could accept the freedom He offered.

" 'Mary has chosen what is better, and it will not be taken away from her' " (Luke 10:42, NIV). Look at the verb conjugation here: good—better—best. What Martha was doing in the kitchen was good. What Mary chose to do by sitting at Jesus' feet was better. If there'd been three or more choices, the Gospel writer would have used the word best to describe Mary's choice.

In my life, it usually isn't a choice of good or better. At any one moment, I have a myriad of activities demanding my attention. How do I choose *which* responsibility I should fulfill *when*? Throw in a generous helping of creative procrastination and my schedule bulges like an aging girdle after Thanksgiving dinner.

Add a touch of ego ("sure, I can handle that!") and I am in serious trouble. My stress level has long since exceeded my IQ (obviously, or I wouldn't be in such a mess). I am ready to blow at the drop of a hat or a shoe or a misspoken word. I needed to learn that my God is the God of stressed-out people. His creative juices flow when His kids turn to Him for rescue.

Money worries? Huh! Temporary cash flow problems in the hands of the Saviour are a joke. He used a fish to satisfy the Jewish IRS and soothe Peter's flagging faith. Talk about creative financing!

Fierce storm clouds on the horizon? Emotional twisters? Teeth-rattling soul quakes? Home-grown hurricanes? Family back drafts? Like Peter, step out of the rickety old boat you built from scrap lumber. Take a walk on the water with your Jesus.

Future myopic? Vision blurred by cataracts of fear? You've lost your depth perception? Turn to your heavenly Ophthalmologist. He didn't mess around healing Bartemaeus' old damaged lenses. He created new eyeballs out of dirt and spit. His lasers of love will not restore your old sight but will give you new sight into His marvelous truths.

Your spirits dead? Your muscles of faith rotting away from your bones? The skeleton of your soul bleaching in the sun of earthly reality? He restored Jairus' daughter. He breathed new life into her collapsed lungs. He unstopped Lazarus's ears. He restored the electrical synapses in his brain. However, turning cynical old Nicodemus into a newborn babe was the greatest miracle of all.

So what are your stressors? What transforms your nerves into static electricity? When faced with scheduling chaos, how do you prioritize your tasks?

To successfully reconnect the wires of sanity in life, learn from Mary. Begin at Jesus' feet. Choosing the best part makes it possible for the better and the good parts of life to become manageable.

Best of all, the moments spent with Jesus can never be taken from you.

# FACE TO FACE WITH FORGIVENESS

# *Section* **3**

# Mary, the Mourner

# CHAPTER NINE

# MY JESUS WILL COME

"Tell Jesus,"—Mary's initial reaction to her brother's illness.

Before the patient took to his bed—"Tell Jesus."

Before the fever spiked—"Tell Jesus."

Before the muscles weakened—"Tell Jesus."

Before the system refused sustenance—"Tell Jesus."

Before a coma replaced reason—"Tell Jesus."

Before the rattle of death sounded—"Tell Jesus."

*"Before they call, I will answer; and while they are yet speaking, I will hear"*
(Isaiah 65:24, KJV).

Before the crisis, Mary turned to her one source of hope and strength. She knew, within her heart, that once Jesus heard the news of His friend's illness, He would rush to Bethany and heal her brother.

Mary's faith wasn't based on emotion or fantasy. If she'd learned anything since her heart transplant, she knew the Source of her strength and the Answer to all her questions. She'd seen scores of people restored with only a touch of the Healer's hands or a word from His mouth.

Whether or not the thought "After all our family has done for the Master, opening our home to Him and His ragtag entourage, how could He refuse?" ever entered her mind, I do not know. Nor does it matter. Mary knew and did what was important. She turned to Jesus.

I can see Martha packing a lunch for the messenger while Mary instructed him a third or a fourth time. "Remember, you must go directly to the Messiah. Don't trust one of the disciples to tell Him. They might forget. They might believe the message not important enough to deliver. Tell Him . . ."

Perhaps, after seeing the messenger off, Mary straightened the parlor or changed the sheets on the guest bed, singing to herself as she worked, knowing that the Master would soon arrive. And Martha—Martha would have rushed to Lazarus's bed to assure the ailing man that the message had been sent. Jesus was coming soon. Only a matter of time and he'd be made well. A matter of time . . .

Time heals all wounds . . .
You'll forget, in time . . .
You'll feel differently, in time . . .
He'll change, in time . . .
It won't matter, in time . . .
It's high time!
There's no time!
There is a time for everything.
Time, always time.

As a child, I had extensive dental work done. I remember one time when my dentist deadened my pain and my consciousness with "laughing gas." I half awoke and found myself trapped in the dentist's chair with all those contraptions holding my mouth open and not a soul in sight. I couldn't move my head. I couldn't get up out of the chair. While I could hear distant voices, eerie and nonsensical, I could see no one. My situation was anything but funny. I was not laughing. Tears slipped down my cheeks, but no one was there to notice. As what seemed like hours trickled past, a claustrophobic fear grew within me, an unreasonable terror. I didn't understand it; I merely responded to it.

My heart raced. I couldn't breathe. I heard a painful wail fill the room—my voice. My hands flew to my face, clawing at the contraptions affixed to my mouth. Before I could do any damage, strong hands grabbed mine and pinned them to the armrests on the chair. A human face stared into mine. I recognized the dental assistant. "Kay! Kay! Stop it. You're all right. Stop it!" Her voice softened when she recognized the terror in my eyes and the tears coursing my cheeks. "You're safe, honey. You're all right."

My eyes darted back and forth. I made several guttural sounds in an effort to be understood.

"Don't worry," she continued, "the doctor will be right back. He's on the phone in the next room. He'll be here any minute." The woman continued to press my forearms into the gray leather armrests while I fought to regain my freedom.

Later, after the dental paraphernalia was removed from my mouth, I learned that the dentist had only been gone for five minutes and that his assistant had never left the room. I was never alone or in danger. I couldn't believe them until I looked at my watch and discovered they were right. I hadn't been in the dentist's office for very long at all. Those five minutes of terror were the longest I've ever lived, before or since. The fear of being confined still pops up in my mind frequently, and I must struggle to control the unreasonable desire to abandon all reason. My mind determines the level of fear and the time element involved.

Time is like that for us humans, speeding and slowing in opposite and adverse proportions to the pleasure or lack of pleasure in one's situation. An entire night can zip by on wings of enjoyment if I have a great book to read while a thirty-second earthquake tremor seems to continue for several minutes.

The hours dragged by for the two sisters. Jesus did not come. Lazarus weakened, and Jesus did not come. A day passed, then two, and Jesus did not come. They knew that the Teacher couldn't be further than a day away, anywhere in Judea.

While others began to doubt that the Saviour would arrive in time to help, Mary stuck to her belief. "He will come tomorrow. Jesus will save my brother's life. I know He will." Yet, Jesus did not come the next morning or at midday or by sunset.

The night vigil began. The sisters kept watch with Lazarus as he weakened further. I can see Martha placing cold, wet towels on Lazarus's forehead, trying to keep down the man's temperature; I can see Mary sitting at the foot of the bed twisting and untwisting her handkerchief, mumbling, "He will come. I know He'll come."

Toward morning, in those incredibly dark hours before dawn, the end came for Lazarus. His last breath escaped his lungs. He was dead. And Jesus hadn't come.

Mary's faith in the intervention of Jesus for her brother hits too close to home for many of us. When my father lay on his deathbed, cancer ravaging his strength and manhood, my mother stoutly maintained, "God will heal Norman. I know He will. He will use Norman's illness as a way to glorify His name to your Uncle Bill." The resoluteness on her face would have been enough to convince my sister and I that she had to be right. "God knows that your Uncle wouldn't listen to reason under any other circumstance. Yes, I know God will heal your father!"

Even during that long night, with the family surrounding my father's bed, my mother refused to consider that God might have another plan. And who of us would have challenged her claims? Mama wasn't a woman to be challenged.

Morning arrived. Our vigil ended, along with my father's pain. My heart stirred at the peace I saw on his tired face. The ambulance took him, accompanied by my mother, to the hospital and declared him dead-on-arrival.

When my brother-in-law brought my mother back from the hospital, I could see that the calm, tranquil expression my mother had worn for so many months had been replaced with a cold empty stare. My father hadn't been healed in the way my mother prayed. My uncle didn't get to "see" the evil of his ways and come to Jesus as a result of my father's miraculous healing. My mother's faith had not been honored. And she couldn't understand why.

What my mother couldn't understand and so many of us fail to grasp is this: God does answer our prayers with a resounding Yes! But in His time.

He is our Healer, whether He chooses to heal instantly, in what we call a miraculous healing, or whether He chooses to let the natural defenses of the body do the healing or if He heals through the skills of modern medicine (both equally as miraculous as the instantaneous healing) or if He chooses to heal at the resurrection. For the Christian, death is a relief, a rest as well. My father's death was, in God's hands, a healing. I know that my father will awaken from the dust with a whole and healthy body. There'll be no lingering trace of cancer, of pain, of wasted muscle,s or of sallow, empty eyes.

My faith comes in accepting the wisdom of God to choose which healing to use on each of His precious children. My trouble begins when I think I know better than God as to what should be done for my loved one.

I know that's easy to say when I am not standing directly over my child's casket or my mate's grave site. However, if I exercise my faith muscles every day in the small crises that try to trip me up, I'll be ready when the Holy Spirit pumps spiritual "Gatorade" into my body when the big crisis arrives. " 'My grace is sufficient for you, for my power is made perfect in weakness' " (2 Corinthians 12:9, NIV).

I imagine, as the two sisters prepared Lazarus's body for burial, they wondered why Jesus hadn't come to Lazarus's rescue. The Scriptures say that many friends and relatives had come from Jerusalem to mourn the passing of Lazarus, since Bethany was less than two miles from the capital city.

Did the mourners wonder if Jesus' failure to appear was due to a fear of the Sanhedrin? Did they apply other motives to His tardiness? No doubt, Jesus' absence was the lead topic of conversation, both to and behind Mary and Martha's backs. When Mary's resolution died with her brother, the mourners noted the change in her demeanor.

I imagine that a similar coldness to my mother's filled Mary's heart—pushing back a thousand unanswered questions she longed to ask, each beginning with the word *why*?

# CHAPTER TEN

# "WHY ME, LORD?"

***"Mary stayed at home"***
(John 11:20, NIV).

Since before the days of Job, human beings when facing troubles have asked God why. For most of us, the question why includes the pronoun me—as in "Why me, Lord?" Even when praying for a loved one, more often than not, our prayers are focused on ourselves in one way or another. With our attention so myopic, we see only our own pain-filled world. We fail to catch a glimpse of the bigger picture, the one that God sees. And in our limited wisdom, we point out to God the advantages of fulfilling our requests in our ways, of aligning His will with ours.

How juvenile. Job's world seemed so limited when the Lord pointed out the extent of God's responsibilities. But, you may say, "I can't see beyond my pain right now."

When I face a tragedy or a problem too big for me to handle, I've found a text that sees me through until my reason returns. Maybe it will help you as well. I discovered it when I was suffering from a devastating disappointment. It was as if my entire life had been stolen from me.

One night when I was lamenting my miserable life, the Holy Spirit led me to Revelation 3:11: "Hold on to what you have, so that no one will take your crown" (NIV).

A steely defiance grew inside my heart. "The people who harmed me, who tried to destroy me, have taken enough," I reasoned. "I can't let them steal my crown as well." God used my fury to get me through the crisis.

You see, I recognized my enemies, both the human and the superhuman ones. I never mistook God as the source of my pain. By turning my anger on the correct source, my anger became a positive tool for healing. The lesson has stayed with me through all kinds of difficulties.

Strange, isn't it, that I seldom ask, "Why me, Lord?" when good fortune shines my way? "Why did you bring this fabulous man into my life, to love me?" It's more likely I'll ask God why I lost my three babies than to ask Him, "Why me, Lord? Why did You bless me with two beautiful and healthy daughters?"

As He dealt with Job and with Mary, God seldom answers my questions directly. God never desired to become my cosmic encyclopedia or my fact-finding Internet™ web page. Jesus came to reveal God the Father, not to reveal easy answers for life's nasty little problems. God is eager to reveal His true self to me, but His image gets all scrambled when my "I" sight needs correcting, when I need spiritual "eye salve" to repair the damage sin has done to my vision. Mary's vision was too narrow as well. All she could see was her precious brother dead, when Jesus could have prevented that from happening. Whether or not Mary asked "Why?" we don't know, but we do know she was angry. For when Martha heard that Jesus had entered Bethany, she went out to meet Him. Mary chose to stay at home.

For Mary not to run to Jesus the moment He arrived sent a message not only to Jesus and to Martha, but also to the mourners gathered at the house. They knew the story of Mary's past and her conversion. They'd watched her. And they had their doubts about the Man she and her family called the Messiah.

Our doubts do the same. They announce to the world, to the universe, in fact, that we don't truly believe Jesus Christ is Lord of lords, that He is faithful to keep His promises, that He can be trusted. When we voice our doubts, skeptics wag their heads and snicker at the "gullible" promises such as 2 Corinthians 1:20: "No matter how many promises God has made, they are 'Yes' in Christ. And so through him the 'Amen' is spoken by us to the glory of God" (NIV).

"Right!" they snort, echoing the accusation spoken throughout time by the father of lies. "There must be a catch, somewhere." Doubt, anger, rejection are all part of Satan's strategy to separate us from our Saviour.

Death clouded Mary's judgment. Initially, she cried, "Tell Jesus." When He didn't come through for her in the way she believed He should, Mary's anger blotted out her faith and obliterated her praise. She couldn't understand why He allowed her brother to die. But soon she would understand. Soon she would be praising again.

But, for the moment, her faith floundered; her strength drained.

Nehemiah 8:10 says, "The joy of the Lord is your strength" (KJV). Mary's anger made her weak. How quickly my praise stops and my joy disappears when troubles come. It makes sense that it would. You see, Satan is a liar. He urges me to whine, gripe, and complain when confronted with a problem. He says, "Kay, your situation is hopeless. God has abandoned you. He doesn't really care." Depression follows discouragement, and my joy is gone.

When Satan manages to destroy my joy, He depletes my strength at the same time. Joy is the last thing he wants me to experience. A fleeting, Disneyland-type happiness? Possibly. But soul-stirring joy? Absolutely not.

The joy that accompanies my praise to God is a joy Satan once knew but will never experience again. He hates knowing that it is mine for the taking. He hates knowing that my praises will take me out of his grasp and empower me with a divine strength. This is a truth the evil one doesn't want me to understand. For when I finally grasp it, he will lose control over my emotional being, where he can cause me to reject the only real source of strength and comfort available to me.

Yet the question hanging in the air for believers and cynics alike in Bethany that day had not yet been answered. Why did Jesus wait to come to Lazarus's aid? He knew and understood the deadly direction the man's illness would take. He felt every pain the man suffered. He knew the moment Lazarus stopped breathing. Nothing could happen to Lazarus that God didn't already know about long before the messenger arrived.

Why? Most of the time, the answer to this question God leaves unanswered. But in the story of Lazarus, the answer soon becomes evident within the story line itself. The answer? To glorify the Father, in His time. There would be no doubt but that the glory belonged to God and God alone.

If Jesus had rushed to Lazarus's side and healed him instantly, the story of the healing would have circulated throughout the community and the glory of God would have been demoted to nothing more than a juicy tidbit of gossip.

If Jesus had waited until Lazarus was near death, the results would have been the same. If the Saviour had come immediately upon His death and restored His life, there would have been room for doubt. "Maybe Lazarus was only in a coma." The miracle would have been diminished. No, God's timing was vital to emphasize the magnitude of Jesus' miracle for that particular time and place in the world's history.

God's timing again. Mary couldn't grasp it, and I, too, miss it so often. Over the years, I've fretted and I've stewed, I've fussed and I've complained, but God is God. He's never too early; He's never too late, but He does wait until the last possible moment, when there can be no doubt but that the glory belongs to God and to God alone.

When Jesus announced to His disciples that "Our friend, Lazarus sleeps. I am going to waken him," the disciples didn't understand.

"He must be doing better," they replied.

"Lazarus is dead." What a devastating announcement

for Jesus to make. Without being at the bedside, Jesus knew the moment His friend had died. Then He waited four days longer. Four days so there'd be no doubt that God is God, and to Him alone belongs the glory.

God would be glorified despite the apparent tragedy, or perhaps, through the tragedy. The miracle Jesus was about to perform would see His disciples through the dark days that would soon follow. The memory of Lazarus's resurrection would buoy their faith when all they had to hold onto was their faith.

Why do I question God's perfect timing? The disciples spent nine hours of terror on a storm-swept lake before Jesus invited Peter to walk on the water with Him. The crippled man at the Gate Beautiful waited five years before receiving his miracle. The Master must have passed his way many times in the three and a half years of His ministry, yet never healed him. But, in God's right time, when Peter and John healed him, the man's leaping and shouting attracted a crowd. Five thousand came to know Jesus as a result, and God's name was glorified. That's God's perfect timing.

I don't have to understand God's timing to submit to it. As a child of God, it is my job to glorify the Father in all things. When I seek God's hand in all things, I can trust that He will work out His will in my life, in His time. I never need to become anxious or fretful.

My faith becomes evident through my praise.

And trust becomes a constant through my experiences.

# CHAPTER ELEVEN

# MARTHA'S REDEMPTION

*"When Martha heard that Jesus was coming, she went out to meet him, but Mary stayed at home"*
(John 11:20, NIV).

Martha is often remembered for her impatience with Mary when she wanted help in the kitchen. But obviously, she hadn't missed everything the Teacher taught. Here, she shines. As soon as she heard of Jesus' arrival, she hurried to meet Him. She was no less disappointed about her brother's death than Mary, yet she hurried to the Master. As usual, outspoken Martha greeted Him with " 'Lord. . . if you had been here, my brother would not have died.' " She hastened to add, " 'But I know that even now God will give you whatever you ask' " (John 11:21, 22, NIV).

Her faith shines through her grief. She declares Jesus to be Christ, the Son of God. No hesitation, despite her grief. In answer to Martha's faith, Jesus reveals to her, " 'I am the resurrection and the life. He who believes in me will live, even though he dies; and whoever lives and believes in me will never die. Do you believe this?' "

(verses 25, 26, NIV).

The sum and substance of the gospel, given to this woman of faith, would be the promise claimed by millions of grieving widows, orphans, husbands, mothers, fathers, and children throughout time until He returns. "I am the resurrection and the life."

The miracle here is that Martha claimed and affirmed Jesus Christ before she had evidence to His validity. She had no manifestation of His power at this point. Her brother's body still lay rotting in the grave. Yet, she believed and praised Him as the Messiah.

The story continued with Martha hurrying back to her younger sister. She found Mary surrounded by mourners.

The mourning described in John 11 is more than quiet weeping like one would see at gravesides in the Western world. The word *weeping* used here denotes a loud wailing like one often sees at funerals in Middle Eastern cultures. Such wailing would blot out whatever deep thinking one might be inclined to do.

Imagine what it's like to be surrounded by wailing mourners. By harbingers of hopelessness. By carriers of cynicism. By devotees to despair. Nothing's worse than to be surrounded by "friends" whose influence produces doubt instead of faith and discouragement in place of encouragement. Their negativism greases the spiral of death until all hope is destroyed.

Wisely, Martha called her sister aside and said, "The Teacher is here and He's asking for you." And wisely, Mary excused herself from the midst of the mourners and ran to Him. *The Message* paraphrase puts it like this, "The moment she heard that, she jumped up and ran out to Him" (verse 29).

I like that! She *ran* to Jesus. A wee snippet of faith, deep within Mary's heart, remained in spite of her grief. That's all it takes sometimes—a small fragment of faith, planted in the heart by the Holy Spirit. That faith was planted during the hours she sat at Jesus' feet—listening, waiting, loving. Buried deep within her heart, it carried her through this dreadful time of pain and doubt.

The fact that Mary ran to Jesus the moment she learned He'd asked for her makes me suspicious that she wasn't aware of His arrival when Martha went to Him. Somehow in the hullabaloo of mourning (it had been going on for four days), she failed to receive the message. But as soon as Mary knew Jesus was near and was asking for her, she ran to Him. She didn't worry about the mourners and what they might think; she just ran. She didn't pause to consider proper funeral protocol; she just ran. She ran and fell at His feet.

This is hardly the picture of a petulant child nursing a grudge. She fell at His feet and wept. Her greeting matched that of her sister's. Obviously, the two sisters had shared their disappointment at the death of their brother. With quivering lips, she sobbed, " 'Lord, if you had been here, my brother would not have died' " (verse 32).

I wonder if this greeting might have been misunderstood over time? Could Mary's declaration have been one of faith and assurance rather than accusation? Could both of the women have been saying, "Lord, we know You could have healed Lazarus if you'd been here." The emphasis could have been on "You" instead of on "could have healed."

Had Jesus been in the sickroom, Lazarus would not have died. She was indeed right. Satan's power would have been thwarted in the presence of the Son of the Living God. What a declaration of faith!

Yet, Christ was with them. He suffered every pain with His friend, Lazarus. His heart wept every tear with the two sisters. Jesus said, "For your sakes . . ." For the sake of His disciples, including Martha and Mary and Lazarus. And it includes those of us who reach out to God during our greatest moments of discouragement, who will have nothing but our faith upon which to rely.

The mourners, thinking Mary was going to the grave site, followed her to Jesus. Mary must have longed to spend a few quiet moments with Jesus. Instead, she found herself surrounded by the wailing mourners. Quiet moments with the Master would have to wait. What she needed most would have to be postponed until another time.

Mary fell at His feet, weeping. Jesus gazed at the crying woman then at the mourners, and He was "deeply moved." *The Message* paraphrase says, "When Jesus saw her sobbing and the Jews with her sobbing, a deep anger welled up within him" (John 11:31).

Anger? Why would He become angry? Was He angry at the mourners for their lack of faith? Angry that they were mourning the loss of Lazarus when before them stood the Source of all life?

Why anger? Somehow, anger doesn't seem appropriate here, especially coming from the Son of God. How could a perfect Being become angry?

Somewhere in my upbringing, anger was considered a sin. I was taught to control (hide) it at all costs. It wasn't until many years into adulthood that I discovered that anger is a perfectly acceptable human emotion. It's what I *do* with my anger that determines whether or not it becomes a sin.

Just as disappointment becomes a sin when I nurse it into discouragement and depression, so anger becomes a sin when it is released into what my mother used to call a "hissy fit." You've seen it happen—someone loses control, and everything and everyone within a thirty-foot range is under attack.

Yet, anger properly harnessed can produce marvelous changes in the world. The driving force of many reforms began with anger. It took one very angry mother to begin the organization MADD, Mothers Against Drunk Drivers. A grieving and angry father began the campaign to pass the "three-strikes-and-you're-out initiative."

But Jesus angry? The Son of God? Perhaps He was angry at pretense of some of the mourners. Perhaps He could see that in only a few days these same sympathizers would be plotting the life of the resurrected Lazarus and His own.

Perhaps His anger originated on a broader, more cosmic level. He saw the grief of these people whom He loved so much. He felt their pain. A fury burned within Him toward Satan, His archenemy, the source of all death and despair.

Life on planet Earth wasn't meant to be this way. Death, while the end was known from the beginning, wasn't part of the agenda at Creation. The Father and the Son knew before They shaped Adam's stately thighs from the clay beside the river that man would fall. They knew before They sculpted Eve's gentle curves that Their creation would fall. Yet, knowing this, They chose to breathe life into the glorious creation of Their hands.

Yes, anger would be an appropriate emotion for the Creator of the universe that day. To see the unnecessary pain His loved ones were suffering would bring about anger within the One who loved them so. To know that the source for all that pain, and for the pain of those who would follow, would stir the King of love to anger.

Recently, I learned of the death of a young woman, the daughter of a college colleague of mine. She was found murdered in her apartment. I felt sorrow for the parents' loss, but more than sorrow, I felt angry. Furious over the rampant crime in our cities. Furious with the easy access criminals have to weapons. Furious with the drug dealers who enslave sniveling druggies, forcing them to steal, maim, and kill to satisfy their addictions. Furious with the satanic forces that create and stimulate such havoc.

What did Jesus do with His anger? Preach a scathing sermon on the "wages of sin"? Deliver a soliloquy on the futility of life? No, He acted on His anger by asking a question. "Where did you put him?"

# CHAPTER TWELVE

# FIRST, HE WEPT

*"Jesus wept"*
(John 11:35, KJV).

Jesus wept. What a sight it must have been to see the Creator of the universe weep. To weep, just like me! Tears trickled down His dusty cheeks. His sinuses swelled. His eyes reddened. His breath caught. His heart ached.

Even though Jesus knew the outcome of the day, He wept. Even though He knew that in a few moments, the mourners would be leaping and shouting for joy, Jesus wept. Even though Satan and his hoary host would soon be forced to give up one of their captives, the Saviour wept. Not from discouragement. Not from grief. But from compassion for all those who would say goodbye to loved ones at gravesides throughout history. He felt their pain, and He wept.

When the mourners saw Jesus weep, they raised their mourning to new heights. The sound of wailing and weeping filled the air. The musicians played their dirges.

# First, He Wept

The drummers pounded their drums. And the singers sang their songs of woe.

Aloud, the mourners said, "Look how much He loved Lazarus."

Others murmured, "If this Man could have opened the eyes of the blind man, couldn't He have kept Lazarus from dying?"

He read their thoughts and understood. As the Saviour stood before the rough-hewn granite slab, He must have had thoughts like, "This isn't the way it was supposed to be, Father. This isn't the way We planned for our children to live. They were made to live forever. No death. No parting. No separation."

As He faced the stone that sealed Lazarus's tomb, Jesus could see ahead to His own death, but a short time away. His death would end death for His children. They would still pass through "the shadow of death," but death itself, the final destruction, would never be able to touch them again.

Finally, Jesus turned to Martha. "Remove the stone."

"Master?" She looked stunned. Out of the corner of her mouth, the woman must have hissed, "He's been dead for four days. He'll stink!"

Jesus must have smiled to Himself. He came to this world from a perfect environment where the perfume of peace wafted on the breeze of love. To the pure Son of God, everything about this foul planet stank. The stench of death and disease hung over the populace like a Los Angeles smog in August. Yet He loved so much He came anyway.

It stinks. A newly graduate medical intern lovingly washes the gnarled and infected feet of an indigent. It stinks, but he does it anyway.

It stinks. The wife of an eighty-year-old Alzheimer's victim changes another soiled diaper. It stinks, but someone has to do it.

It stinks. A teenager holds her drunken mother's head while the woman vomits up her night of partying. It stinks, but love compels her to continue her caretaking.

It stinks. A loyal friend bathes the AIDS patient's festering sores. It stinks, but the weak smile he receives is worth it.

It stinks. A father stands beside the grave of his slain son. It stinks and nothing on this side of eternity can make it better.

It stinks. Bad breath. Body odor. Sour vomit. Infested hair. Putrefied flesh. Rotting teeth. Oozing wounds. Decomposing body.

It stinks. Rancid dreams. Gangrenous promises. Disintegrating relationships.

It stinks. Sin and the results of sin stink. And only the Son of the Living God can remove the stench of sin and death and replace it with the clean, pure aroma of eternal life.

When Martha protested, Jesus turned to her. "Didn't I tell you that if you believed, you would see the glory of God?"

Martha must have swallowed hard, but she obeyed. Her eyes filled with tears; she gave the signal for the servants to remove the stone. And Jesus prayed aloud.

" 'Father, I thank you that you have heard me. I knew that you always hear me, but I said this for the benefit of the people standing here, that they may believe that you sent me' " (John 11:41, NIV).

Father. He began by addressing His Father, giving the God of the universe His just due. There was no begging or pleading, just a simple Thank You for hearing His prayer. So often I pray as if I expect God to refuse my request. I beg and plead, wail and cajole, much like the prophets of Baal did around Elijah's altar, as if my frenzy and my tears will alter the Divine Mind.

"Ask" as the Master said; then thank the Father for what He said He'd do. "Thank You, Father, for glorifying Your name through my request."

The dog barked, and my daughters whirled in circles around the living room. "We're going to Disneyworld," they shouted. "We're going to Disneyworld." The family had been discussing summer vacation plans that included going to Orlando, Florida, to see Grandma.

Always quick to pick up on an opportunity, Rhonda asked, "Can we visit Disneyworld while we're there?"

Richard grinned and nodded. "I'm sure we can fit Disneyworld into our vacation plans."

They didn't need to ask a second time to be certain they'd heard their father right. Without hesitation, they were off, doing their jig of celebration. During the weeks that followed, they chose the clothes they'd take, the toys they couldn't leave behind, even the rides they'd go on first. But never in those days previous to our departure did they go to their father and ask, "Daddy, are you sure we are going to Disneyworld? Do you really mean it?"

While they talked incessantly about the upcoming adventure, they didn't doubt their father's word for a minute. Over the years, they'd come to trust him. They knew he kept his promises.

My heavenly Father keeps His promises as well. When we make a request in prayer for a friend or ourselves and we pray that through everything God's name will be glorified, we align ourselves with the Father's will. Aligned with the Father's will, our prayers are answered Yes in Jesus Christ (Remember? 2 Cor. 1:20, NIV).

Begging isn't necessary. I must come boldly to the Father's throne, not because of my worthiness, but because of Jesus' sacrifice. As God's child, I have that right, that privilege, to come to the Father in the dignity of Jesus Christ.

A photographer snapped a picture of Caroline Kennedy and one of her friends playing dolls under the front lip of the desk in the President's Oval Office. In an office where statesmen and leaders trembled to visit, two little girls dressed their dolls. Caroline knew her daddy. Even though her father was the most powerful man in the world, she wasn't afraid. First, he was her daddy.

God, the Emperor of the universe, is first, our Daddy. He chose to become our Father when He and His Son Jesus created the world. That's when He said, "Let's make man in our image." That's when He became our Dad. That's when man gained the privilege of approaching the universe's "Oval Office."

Caroline Kennedy didn't have to beg for her father's favor. And I doubt that she ever begged her father to "go easy" on Fidel Castro. Her purpose in life wasn't to affect international policy but just to be his daughter.

Prayer isn't for changing the mind of God but for aligning me with the mind of God. Jesus knew He was in the will of His Father. He didn't have a doubt in the world or in the world to come. He thanked the Father for hearing His request even before the miracle happened. That's confidence in the Father.

He did this aloud so the people would hear and understand, especially those who loved Him. He didn't want any misunderstandings as to the Source of the miracle.

Jesus gave me an example for giving God the glory, aloud, vocally, so the faith of others may be strengthened. There have been times I've hesitated to do so, afraid that someone might misunderstand my message. But Jesus' example shows me that I can never give God too much glory for what He does for me.

# CHAPTER THIRTEEN

# "LET THERE BE LIGHT"

*"The earth was formless and void, and darkness was over the surface of the deep; . . . Then God said, 'Let there be light;' and there was light"* (Genesis 1:2, 3, NASB).

I'd never felt such darkness, and *feel* is the correct word. I stood in a group of school children in the bowels of Howe's Cavern in New York. Our guide turned out all the lights, leaving us in total darkness, a palpitating darkness, a cloying darkness.

Forty years later, the experience of that darkness still sends cold chills down my spine and causes me to breathe in short, hysterical gasps. I still avoid dark, close places. Until I smelled, tasted, and, yes, heard the sounds of complete darkness, I couldn't begin to understand darkness.

Darkness permeated the atmosphere inside the cave where Lazarus lay. A deeper, denser darkness than what I experienced in the caverns. The darkness in Lazarus's tomb not only lacked the presence of light but also the presence of Light. When I was underground experiencing my moment of total darkness, God was with me. No child of God can ever be in total darkness as long as the Source of all light is there. Unlike Lazarus, I wasn't being held captive by the prince of darkness.

In Lazarus's cave, the hollow dirge of death sang of victory. The demons danced in demented delight. And the despot of doom draped himself across the foot of the stone slab concealing the body of God's faithful servant and admired his perfectly manicured claws. However, in his moment of glory, his throes of victory, old slew-foot forgot one very important moment in time.

"In the beginning, God . . ." Out of a formless mass of nothing, He created the world. Yet, there was darkness over the surface of the deep. Utter, outer darkness.

The Hebrew word for this darkness, *choshek*, means the complete opposite of God-light. That was the darkness filling the nooks and crannies of the dusty cave outside the city limits of Bethany that day. That's the extent of darkness whenever the prince of darkness is allowed to take control.

Darkness is an interesting phenomenon. It can only exist in the absence of light. The instant light appears, darkness must flee. For darkness to leave isn't open to discussion, to argument, or to debate. It must flee.

Didn't the force of darkness remember the moment the Creator announced "Let there be light"? Didn't he recall how he and his imps had fled that pure, beautiful light of creation? Apparently not. Did Lucifer, once the angel of light forget, that a few days earlier Jesus said "I am the Light of the world"? Either he forgot or didn't believe.

Because, at that moment, outside the little hillside cave, while the prince of darkness reveled in his victory in darkness, the Prince of Light stood ready to wrest His friend from the clutches of the evil one.

Both beings knew there would be another battle in a few short days. Today this would be the dress rehearsal. They would face off again at Calvary. All of the universe leaned forward in their royal seats to watch as the Son of Man broke the chains of death for one of God's servants.

The pawn in this cosmic drama lay on the rough-hewn rock ledge, near where his parents and grandparents had been placed years earlier, near the spots where his sisters would one day join him. Dead. Jesus called it sleeping. God's Word describes it as rest.

What was Lazarus's first thought? Did he see the light flowing in from outside the tomb? Is that what awakened him from his death slumber? What made him, bound in funeral clothes, open his eyes, sit up, stand to his feet? The light shining in from the cave's opening?

What sent life's electric currents through Lazarus's brain once more, what caused new blood to surge through his veins, what caused his heart to resume beating, was not the light. The light only chased the darkness. The voice of Jesus broke through the barriers of death and freed Lazarus.

It was the Voice.

"In the beginning was the Word" (John 1:1, KJV). Right from the start, the Word, the Creator of the world, spoke His commands. Four thousand years later, the Creator stood outside the walls of Lazarus's tomb and demonstrated His creative voice again.

His simple words, "Lazarus, come out," moved heaven and earth. His command was heard in the deepest bowels of the earth. His voice echoed to the most distant planets in the universe.

"Lazarus, come out."

Did the Creator arrest the decay occurring within Lazarus's body? Did He rejuvenate the circulatory system? Did He reassemble the DNA cells? Or did Jesus as Creator bring about a new Lazarus from the dust of Bethany as He did from the dust of Eden?

All I know for certain is when Jesus called for His friend to come forth, Lazarus came forth—bound and gagged like a mummy, according to the burial customs of the land and times. No hesitation. No questioning. No doubt. No fear. Once the Master's words escaped His lips, the miracle occurred. Life flowed once again within the dead man. And all the demons of hell could not prevent it.

The Word lives Eternal. The Word would prevail at Calvary. The Word will prevail at the Oakwood Cemetery, at the Laurel Cemetery, at any and every cemetery where one of God's children rests secure in His promise. The day will come when Life will call forth new lives from the smoldering ruins of manmade sarcophagi. And all who love Him will hear the Voice. What a promise! What a comfort! What a joy!

What a privilege to know that Jesus doesn't just give life—He is life. To be assured that He doesn't just show us the way—He is the Way. That He doesn't just tell us the truth—He is the truth.

He is our Everything. He is our Saviour.

# CHAPTER FOURTEEN

# TELL ME THE STORY

*"I know he will rise again
in the resurrection at the last day"*
(John 11:24, NIV).

The state of the dead:
Theologians argue . . .
Rock stars sing . . .
Philosophers theorize . . .
Druggies aspire . . .
Poets eulogize . . .
And those in mourning beg for answers.

My husband is a computer nut—an Internet™ junkie. I tease him that he should be grateful evolution doesn't work or his squeaky desk chair would already be adhering to his blue jeans, considering the amount of time he spends in front of the computer screen. My teasing is part exaggeration and part envy—I would like to interact with this modern technology more than I do.

Interact. The word has been revitalized in my vocabulary, thanks to the world of cyberspace. On his PC,

Richard can tap into the Stanford University Library. He can access both Oxford's and the University of Moscow's library facilities—all without leaving his desk chair. He can interact live with famous authors, renowned scientists, and leading theologians by opening the correct door to specific computer meeting rooms.

The traditional walls of communication have crumbled. Richard is not limited by distance or politics. Even time does not slow down his movement. The works of great minds of the past are open for the interested cybertechnician.

If I could travel this miraculous super highway to communicate with Mary and Martha, there are many questions I would love to ask them. This moment in our story, however, belongs to Lazarus. He's the man of the hour, the one with the answers.

And I have so many questions to ask him. Questions upon questions upon questions. What was it like to wake up from death? Did he even realize what had happened?

Can you even imagine Lazarus's experience?

**Lazarus**

"Lazarus, come out!" The Voice broke through my nothingness. Yes, that's right, nothingness. I know of no other way to describe it.

"Where am I?" was my first thought. I didn't recognize my surroundings. My last memory was of being in my bed, with my sisters standing on each side of me, weeping. Martha bathed my forehead with a cool cloth. It felt so good. Ah yes, I remember the pain, the searing pain.

I also remember the weakness. I hated being weak,

needing help to perform my bodily functions. How humiliating. I've always been the strong one in the family, and suddenly my precious sisters were forced to care for my most basic and private needs.

My sister Martha, along with the help of our hired servants, did most of the nursing duties. I wouldn't have expected less from faithful Martha. And dear, sweet Mary, my baby sister, held my hand, reassuring me that Jesus would come. "Hang on a little longer," she repeated over and over again.

I remember thinking that if He didn't arrive soon, it would be too late. I can't explain the knowledge that comes in those last moments, knowing I was about to die. But I knew. And it was simple. As my body grew weaker, I closed my eyes and breathed a deep, peaceful sigh. And then I heard Jesus' voice calling me.

At first, I thought He stood in the doorway of my bedroom. "He's here." I wanted to shout my welcome. "You made it in time!" I couldn't understand why my bedclothes were so tight and constricting and why Martha had placed a square of linen over my face. I needed air. "What could she have been thinking?" I wondered.

Then I knew the truth. This wasn't my bedroom; it was the family tomb. It wasn't my bedding constricting me; it was my graveclothes. And the linen facecloth wasn't placed to block my breathing, for I had no breath to block. I was dead. At least, I was until I heard that Voice.

"So this is what it's like to die. Will I go to heaven wearing these graveclothes?" I wondered. I knew heaven was mine, not for what I did but for God's promises that would be fulfilled through the Messiah. I sat up and dropped my bound legs over the side of the stone slab. My bare feet touched the dusty floor of the crypt. The light flowing in from the opening of the tomb shined through the facecloth.

Instinctively, I knew I had to walk toward the light. Walking wasn't easy with my legs bound together. I stubbed my toe on a pebble but caught my balance in time. I'd barely inched to the doorway when the Master spoke again. "Unbind him; let him go!"

I heard Martha's voice, hysterically calling out to one of the servants, "Go get my brother's robe and his sandals. Hurry!"

The facecloth slipped from my eyes. All I could see was Jesus' smiling face. I could tell He'd been crying. I wanted to fall to my knees to worship Him, but my graveclothes prevented me from doing so. A thousand hands started removing my wrappings. A robe appeared, and I slipped my arms into the sleeves and wrapped it about my body. I did all this without taking my gaze from His face, His beautiful face.

Freed from all constrictions, I fell to the ground before Him. What else could I do? I had to worship the One who restored me to life. I had to bow before the One who redeemed me from the grave.

Then the party began. So many times over the last few months, I had discovered that when you invite Jesus into your life, a celebration begins. It was true once more. My, what a party we had. But this celebration outstripped any celebration I've ever experienced.

It took a few minutes for the mourners to comprehend what had happened. But when they did, the dirges sung in minor keys switched to majors; the shuffling, grieving feet began to dance. Someone shouted, "Break out the tambourine! Flutists, play your flutes. Lyrists, pick up your lyres. Let's have a party!"

And Jesus and I were right in the middle of the line dance, arm over arm with the other men, kicking our feet into the air to the time of the music. The women also, arm in arm, circled inside the men's larger circle; singing, rejoicing, crying, laughing, and praising all at the same time. The gifts of food and wine supplied for the funeral guests became party fixings. We ate and drank and rejoiced together until the early morning hours. It was incredible. And through it all, I couldn't take my eyes off the Master.

Between the dances and the singing, the questions flowed all night long as well. To be the first man in the community to die and return to talk about it! What did it feel like to die? What did you see on the other side? Did you go anywhere? Did you meet anyone? Did it hurt?

I answered as best I could, but truly, I had little to say. What could I say? One moment I closed my eyes and I could feel Martha washing my forehead with cool water. Then, the next moment I heard my Friend's voice. That was it. That's all there was. The four days my sisters talked about didn't happen to me. It was but an instant, and I heard His voice.

The local rabbi was frustrated that I couldn't produce more information from the "other side," but you can't talk about something that didn't happen. Oftentimes during the interrogations, I'd glance toward Jesus for help and He'd smile and tip His head toward me as if to say, "This is your time, Lazarus. You're doing fine."

Others who had witnessed my resurrection scurried back to Jerusalem to tell members of the Sanhedrin about the Teacher's latest miracle. "This one should set them back on their heels," I thought. They might be able to disregard the healing of blind Bartemaeus or curing the leprosy of Simon—one of their own. But a man brought back to life after four days in the grave? Such a sensation is bound to cause trouble for the Messiah.

Almost two thousand years later, a little boy described Lazarus's experience so well. Throughout the funeral, five-year-old Eric watched his parents mourn the loss of his baby brother, Jeffery. Later, at their home, as friends and family came and went, weeping and comforting the desperate parents, Eric watched. After the last guest left, Eric's mother threw herself across her bed and buried her face in a pillow.

The child crawled upon his parents' bed and patted his mother's arm. "Don't worry, Mama. Someday Jesus is going to give Jeffery new batteries."

While the mysteries of the universe were still a mystery to the young mind, God had spoken to his heart. Death was simple for him to understand. When his toys stopped running, he knew they needed new batteries. Combining that knowledge with his childlike faith, he understood what the sages of time have often missed.

We've worked so hard to explain death that we've nearly buried it under mountains of words. "Forgive us, Father, for trying to make Your truth so complicated, so convoluted, and so obtuse, that we miss the simple beauty that is clear enough for a child to understand."

# FACE TO FACE WITH FORGIVENESS

# *Section*
# 4

# Mary, the Beloved

# CHAPTER FIFTEEN

# COUNTING THE COST

*"A dinner was given in Jesus' honor"*
(John 12:2, NIV).

After the crowds dispersed, Martha announced to the family, "We should have a banquet in honor of what the Teacher has done for you, Lazarus, and what He did for Simon, as well."

Lazarus looked at Martha and nodded. He knew better than to disagree or to point out that they had one of the greatest celebrations possible, right at the grave site. But he knew when Martha got on a "kick," nothing and no one could deter her. So a party there'd be—a banquet, in fact.

I can imagine Mary being enthused at first. Her Saviour would visit again. She'd be able to listen to His stories and learn more about the kingdom. That was before Martha mentioned including Simon the Pharisee in the celebration. Simon, the man who'd lured her, a twelve-year-old child, to his estate and defiled her.

As Mary stood in her sister's kitchen cleaning the grape

leaves for stuffing, she remembered that day too well. The aroma of jasmine in the courtyard. A tray of sweets like she seldom got at home. His words of flattery—"You're so beautiful. Those ebony ringlets, your slim neck, your soft white shoulders." And the bed, the gigantic bed.

Once she discovered the man's intentions, she begged him to stop. She cried. She pleaded. He only laughed and blamed her for luring him with her smiles. She tried to escape. But how does an eighty-pound child flee from a one hundred and seventy pound man?

"No." Mary shook her head. "No, I should have had enough sense not to go with him in the first place. If I'd only stuck to my task of drawing the water for Martha instead of . . ." She'd been so curious about the Pharisee's giant walled estate on the edge of town. Curious. That was the day her curiosity died, along with her dreams. No decent man would marry a marked woman. She had only recourse, and she took it.

And she seldom looked back. Yet, the cancer of hate toward the man nibbled away at her heart. Being with the Master, listening to His words, she knew the hate had to go. Over and over, Jesus taught that the only weapon to fight one's enemies—whether they be the hated Romans or the lascivious Simon—was love and nonviolence.

The Saviour carried out His peace initiative in visible and concrete ways. About the Roman soldiers, He said, " 'If someone forces you to go one mile, go with him two miles' " (Matthew 5:41, NIV). Can you imagine what the Roman soldier would think, expecting a curse and receiving a smile and an offer to carry the load another mile willingly?

Mary heard Jesus say, " 'Do not resist an evil person if

someone strikes you on the right cheek, turn to him the other also' " (Matthew 5:39, KJV). But more importantly, she saw the Messiah live his policy. When Jesus said, "Love your enemies and pray for those who persecute you," He presented more than a theory. He ignited a way of life.

If only more Christians followed His example. It is said that once, someone asked the great peace advocate, Ghandi, his thoughts about Christianity. He replied, "Beautiful, but I've never seen anyone live it."

Both Jesus' words and His example tumbled around in Mary's mind like dust devils in the fallow fields surrounding her home. "How can I apply the principle to my situation?" she must have wondered. No man could understand the shame and the violation she'd felt following the attack.

Whenever she spent time with Jesus, the thoughts niggled at her conscience. When He spoke of repaying violence by love, praying for the well-being of the oppressors, she knew she had to let it go. She had to release the anger and the hatred buried within her soul for over a decade. *But how*, she wondered, *how do I do that? How do I face him right in his own home?*

As she watched Jesus living a life of unconditional love for everyone, she came to realize that He was modeling the Father. "But I tell you: Love your enemies and pray for those who persecute you, that you may be [daughters] of your Father in heaven. He causes his sun to rise on the evil and the good . . ." (Matthew 5:4,5-46, NIV).

Talk about compassion! The sun and the rain fall equally on the just and the unjust, on the good and the bad, on those who love Him and those who hate Him.

That's what finally broke Mary's heart—Christ's compassion and forgiveness. He'd forgiven her so completely; she must now forgive Simon, whether Simon deserved it or not.

Before she slipped away from the kitchen to her room, before she removed the box of coins from its hiding place, before she dropped the money into her purse, Mary counted the cost.

She could not resist God's love. Love for her Saviour welled up within her heart until it consumed all other surmising. Nothing could be more important to her than loving Him. A theory wouldn't do—her all-consuming love prompted action.

Mind, spirit, and body. Love demands all. When I fell in love with my husband, I won't say that I fell in love with his mind first. He had the cutest smile and the brightest twinkle in his eyes when he teased—ah! But after only a few dates, his mind proved to be irresistible. I liked the way he thought. I liked his sense of humor and his reasoning ability. And needless to say, his spirit soon captivated me as well.

When we married and Rhonda, our firstborn, entered our hearts and lives, we, like all new parents, would watch her sleeping in her bassinet and try to decide what physical traits came from where. She had my ears, no doubt. They tipped out at the top, like pixie ears. She had her grandmothers' big blue eyes. As she grew, we discovered she had her daddy's determination. We discovered this the first time we tried to feed her peas! We love every portion of what makes Rhonda Rhonda.

Likewise, God's children inherit His traits, or I should say, the traits of the Godhead. Theologians tell us that our minds—the mind of a child of God—is where we are like

God the Father. The body, they tell us, reveals our likeness to Jesus; the spirit and the emotion comes from the Holy Spirit. Whether or not this is too simplistic to adequately describe the mysterious process of salvation, I can't tell you. But Mary understood that loving Jesus would take her entire self, her mind, her body, and her spirit.

She'd spent her life giving away her body while protecting her mind and her spirit from getting involved. Yet, both had become more sullied with each encounter. Scarred, broken, used, and defiled, she came to Him, and He loved her. In return, she could love completely.

Several years ago the rock musical "Jesus Christ Superstar" hit Broadway. In it, Mary was described as Jesus' courtesan, His "chippy" on the side. The very idea repulses the true child of God because it lessens the Saviour and Mary's relationship. Jesus did for Mary what no other "man" could ever do. He gave to her the one thing she longed for most. The Creator of the universe restored her virginity, her spiritual virginity. He cleansed her mind, body, and soul. How could she help but return her love to Him as completely?

How freeing it is to love so completely! Perhaps that's why the Bible writers refer to the relationship between Christ and the church as a marriage. Jeremiah declares the Lord as our "husband." The closest bond on planet Earth is used to describe the relationship God wants with His people.

It's kind of scary to let go of one's reserves, to bare one's soul, mind, and body. It's risky. Dangerous. We hold back for fear He can't be trusted. And over and over again, He proves He is trustworthy. He is a faithful Spouse and so much more.

# CHAPTER SIXTEEN

# OUTLANDISH GIFTS

*"A woman came to Him with an alabaster jar of very expensive perfume"*
(Matthew 26:7, NIV).

Frieda shook her head in wonder. "What is a baby shower?" Immigrating to a new land meant learning a new language and new customs. When she asked her neighbor about this "baby shower," the neighbor laughed and told her it was a party for a new baby and that a baby gift would be expected.

Frieda shopped for just the right gift. On the day of the shower, she arrived early with her gift in hand. But when she entered the hostess's apartment and saw the stack of brightly wrapped gifts, tied with pretty ribbons of blue, pink, and yellow, Frieda's face blazed with embarrassment.

Awkwardly, she slipped her gift, wrapped in the store's brown bag, beneath the other shower gifts. Throughout the games and the refreshments, Frieda fidgeted nervously. *If only I'd known.* When the new mother began opening the gifts, Frieda's nervousness grew. Finally she opened Frieda's gift.

The mouths of the guests dropped open at the sight of the gift inside the simple brown sack. Frieda's gift, while lacking a wrapping decked with pastel ducks, bunnies, and teddy bears, was, by far, the most expensive present of all, costing twice to three times as much as the gifts wrapped in the fancy paper.

Gift wrapping always delights me. I like brightly wrapped packages! When I receive an attractively wrapped package, it feels like the presenter went to a little extra trouble for me. In reality, the colorful wrappings are nothing more than custom—an American custom. And I must admit, I'd rather have a new silk dress wrapped in a grocery bag than a secondhand cotton house dress inside a Macy's garment box. While the thought is important, the gift does count as well.

Mary knew that the quality of her gift counted. She would use her all to buy the best. Nothing less for her Jesus would do. Imagine with me what it must have been like that day, the day of Simon the Leper's feast.

As she slipped through the silent midday streets of Bethany, she had one destination in mind—the best apothecary shop in town. She must have shopped there often to purchases spices and ointments to please her customers. I can almost see her pausing repeatedly to admire the exquisite bottle of nard on the shelf behind the shopkeeper's head. Perhaps once she inquired of the price. The equivalent of one year's wages—about $35,000 to you and me.

While she might have wished for the rare and exotic fragrance, she knew it would never be the property of a common prostitute. One day, the high falutin' wife of some Pharisee or royal personage would sweep into the tiny shop and snatch the alabaster flask from the shelves. And to such a privileged woman the fragrance wouldn't be special, just another vial to add to her bath collection or to sit on a night table to admire from afar.

A touch of anxiety rushed through Mary as she hurried to the shop the morning of the great feast. Perhaps the bottle had already sold. What then? Settle for second best? She shook the thought from her mind and hurried down the side street to the store.

The bell jangled over her head as she stepped inside the dusty shop. A caged bird called out his greeting. Rows of crystal bottles, alabaster boxes, and brass containers lined the shelves along the walls. A rug from Persia—its reds and blues and greens faded to muted tones—covered the stone floor. Sunlight filtered in through the small open window. The musty smell of chemicals and fragrances hung in the oppressive afternoon air.

But Mary focused her gaze on the hand-carved alabaster flask that held an incredibly expensive perfume. Yes, that was the perfume she wanted. Nothing less would do. The long-necked, sealed flask held the aromatic oil called nard, extracted from a plant grown in India. The alabaster flask allowed the fragrance to seep through a little at a time, like potpourri.

The curtain of colorfully glazed clay beads at the back of the shop rattled. A wiry little man with a thick black beard, a heavy mustache, and a turban on his head brushed the beads aside with his hand and stepped out from behind the beaded curtain. "May I help you?"

Mary smiled and withdrew her cache of funds from

beneath the lapels of her robe. She took a deep breath and set the bulging purse on the small wooden table where the shopkeeper conducted his business. "Yes, you can."

The man squinted at Mary. "I know you. You're the—"

Mary's story had been the talk of the town for several weeks. A reformed prostitute was unheard of. And to think of the Man from Galilee dealing with such people. Before the man could voice his censure, she replied, pointing to the alabaster vial. "I've come to buy your most expensive perfume today."

The man drew his head back in disbelief and snorted. A wry smile lifted one corner of his mouth. His gaze skimmed over her body like a snake slithering along the desert floor. She shivered in disgust.

"The perfume?" She arched one eyebrow in censure.

He grinned hungrily, running his tongue over his brown, rotting teeth. "You can't afford my finest, Missy." He reached for a small wooden flask from beneath the counter. "Now, this one here is more to your . . ."

Mary's lips tightened before she spoke. Her eyes flashed. *Would men's attitudes about her never change*, she wondered. "I'd like the alabaster flask with the nard, please." Her fingers tapped her leather drawstring purse that contained her hard-earned coins.

The man's lust shifted from the former prostitute's body to her bulging purse. He moistened his lips with his tongue. "Hmm," he muttered, "The alabaster vial, is it? Important engagement tonight? VIP from Jerusalem?"

Mary stiffened, then leveled her gaze at him. "The perfume?"

He stared at the purse for several seconds, trying to

gauge just how much money he could milk out of this customer. He reached for the flask and set it on the table between them. "As you can see, the intricate carvings on the vial alone are worth more than a hundred denarii. And then the fragrance, nothing like it grown in all Judea. It's shipped in from India, you know."

"How much are you asking for it?"

"Uh, let's see now. A woman in your position . . ." He snickered at his shady innuendo. His eyes narrowed. "Hmm. Seven hundred denarii."

People were always underestimating Mary, especially men. Without loosening the drawstrings on her purse, she answered, "Two hundred fifty denarii."

The shopkeeper snorted. "Six hundred."

"Four hundred."

"Five hundred and no less."

"Sold."

Mary didn't hesitate about purchasing the gift. She'd counted the cost. Willing, eager, she stacked the coins on the rough oak table in front of the shopkeeper's greedy gaze. He rubbed his hands together in anticipation as the woman counted aloud.

While the shopkeeper recounted the money, Mary gazed at the stacks of coins on the table, her entire savings from a life of self-degradation. She'd saved the money to sustain herself through old age.

She spent the equivalent of a year's salary. She would have spent two years of earnings, three years even, for her Master. She loved Him so much.

She had counted the cost of forgiveness. She had counted the cost of eternal life. And it was worth everything she had.

# CHAPTER SEVENTEEN

# EXCUSE ME

*"She pre-anointed my body for burial"*
(Mark 14:8, *The Message*).

The Master's strange words lately disturbed Mary. They sounded like warnings, warnings of death. Destroy the temple? Sacrifice My body? She couldn't understand. When she voiced her concerns to her siblings, they scoffed.

"Stop being so fanciful, Mary, dear," Lazarus scolded.

"You and your strange ideas." Martha clicked her tongue. "Do you really think the God of the universe would allow a few members of the Sanhedrin to assassinate His Son?" Lazarus reasoned. "Jesus is here to set up God's kingdom on this earth. He's getting ready to raise an army and . . ." Lazarus could wax eloquent on the subject of defeating the Romans.

"Yes," Martha would add, "and your brother is sure to be chosen to be on His cabinet, as he and Jesus are such good friends."

"Mary, think," Lazarus drawled, "if you are right, don't you think Peter and John would be talking about it too? Face it, you've been through a troublesome time, and your mind is overtaxed, that's all. You're seeing ghosts behind every fish stand and goblins under every pomegranate bush."

The woman bowed her head. *He's probably right*, she thought. Yet, she couldn't shake her foreboding. The conflict raged within her as she helped her sister prepare the food for the evening banquet. *Am I mistaken?* she wondered. *If I'm not, why doesn't anyone else see it?* She prayed she was wrong, but in her heart, she knew she wasn't.

She knew the mood of the Jerusalem Pharisees. She'd heard the rumors out of the temple. And then, Jesus' own words. In her family parlor, she'd heard Jesus predict His own death; she was sure of it.

She bought the precious nard to express her deep devotion for her Saviour. Her gratitude demanded some unusual sign of her affection. She felt a burning love in her heart that could not be contained. This Man, Jesus, accepted and forgave her when no other human being would dare touch her—in public at least—for fear of contamination.

Now, would her gift be needed to anoint His body for burial? She shivered, an effort to push the ugly idea from her mind.

Being a woman, I can guarantee that Mary chose her garments carefully that evening. I can see her holding up several dresses in front of her bedroom mirror. This one? No, too uncomfortable. This one? Oh no, too daring. This one? Eeugh! Too blue! I need something dark and unobtrusive. She knew her goal, and she would allow nothing to get in her way. Anointing Jesus was all that mattered. She would seize the moment, a moment that may never come again.

I can see her pause in the doorway to the banquet room, her fingers white from clutching her alabaster bottle. I can feel the butterflies in her stomach and the beads of sweat on her forehead. I can taste the dryness in her mouth. Did she wait until Martha was busy filling the serving bowls with couscous or the trays with stuffed grape leaves? Or did she bring her sister into her plans?

Regardless, as she stood in the doorway, beyond the beaded curtains, I imagine her courage flagged. She could see the men reclining around the table as was the custom. The room buzzed with laughter and good conversation. Her skin crawled at the sight of Simon the leper, the host. She gazed at her brother, so full of life and vitality once more, and her spirits soared. Then, in the candlelight, she saw the smiling face of her Saviour and her confidence returned.

Entering the all male feast took courage, but Mary had nothing to lose. Neither did she have anything to gain. Her reputation had been destroyed long ago. She had no one to impress.

"Excuse me," she whispered hesitantly as she stepped over the feet of the man nearest the doorway. He turned and frowned.

"What is a woman doing in here?"

"Must be one of the servers," the man next to him reasoned.

"Excuse me." She inched her way along the shadowy wall.

"Where does she think she's going?" A man hissed, disapproval dripping from his lips.

"Excuse me." Her voice quivered with fear.

"Who does she think she is?"

"Excuse me." She cleared her throat. "Excuse me."

An atmosphere of indignation replaced the earlier camaraderie of the room. Mary said, "Excuse me."

When the laughter turned to scorn, when the tongues wagged, clicked, and hissed, she said, "Excuse me."

She moved through the barriers of censure without being affected by them. "Excuse me." Mary never doubted. No matter what anyone thought, she would anoint Jesus. She gave no apologies. She made no excuses. She voiced no explanations.

"Excuse me." Nothing could deter her. Not the people, not the music, not the order of service, the building, the walls, or the color of the carpet. She would worship her Saviour.

When she arrived at Jesus' feet, His look of approval reminded her of the day He forgave her sins. Tears sprang into her eyes. Any residual fear melted in the warmth of His love. Without a word, she dropped to His feet and broke the alabaster vial.

Mary broke the bottle. The alabaster shards scattered across the wooden floor. With the flask broken, there was no turning back. No reconsideration. No drop-by-drop commitment for Mary. She would give her all. Tears streamed down her cheeks. Gratitude flowed from her like the ointment flowed from the alabaster jar.

The soothing nard spilled onto Jesus' tired feet. The Master inhaled the sweet aroma of her gift. Those closest to Him sniffed the fragrance in the air and looked to its source. Those who hadn't noticed when Mary slipped into the room noticed her now. They saw her remove the combs that held her thick, lustrous ebony-brown hair in place. They watched the curtain of hair, Mary's most precious sign of her womanhood, tumble down, flowing over Jesus' feet as a turkish towel.

If she thought she could slip in, anoint Jesus, and slip out without being noticed, she discovered that would not be the case the moment she broke the flask. The spilled perfume filled the air. The nard permeated the wood flooring and would continue to give off the evidence of Mary's act for days to come.

Wouldn't it be wonderful if the aroma of kindness and compassion lingered wherever Christ's children walked? If love saturated every word and action? Whether in secret or under the world's gaze, the resulting fragrance would be felt. Perhaps then, sincere searchers of truth would see the kingdom of God in action and be irresistibly drawn inside.

Is this kind of love possible in a world like mine, where I deal with car repairs, house payments, orthodontist bills, and the IRS? Where the green arrow at the corner changes to red just as I approach the turn lane? Where no matter which checkout line I choose, the person in front of me needs a price check or wants to cash an employment check far beyond the accepted amount? Where the doctor's office I must visit has books available for their waiting patients instead of magazines—and you have time to finish the one you're reading before you get to see the doctor?

It is possible, praise God! The scent of love revealed in Mary's experience can be mine, and must be mine. If I break the vial, if I spill the precious perfume, if I give my all, as Mary did, my love for my Saviour will permeate through my everyday life.

And through me, it will touch every person I meet. Then every word and deed of mine becomes an invitation to know the Jesus I love.

# CHAPTER EIGHTEEN

# "THE MONEY, LORD"

*" 'Why wasn't this perfume sold*
*and the money given to the poor?' "*
(John 12:5, NIV).

Jesus and the men reclined on couches with their feet extended away from the table. This allowed Mary easy access to the Saviour's feet, to pour the perfume and to wipe it with her hair, and yet not disturb Him. But like the woman in the crowded Judean street who touched His garment and received her healing, Mary's act would not go unnoticed.

I can almost hear my mother's voice. "Secret actions, good or bad, never stay secret. Eventually, they will come to light. They will receive their just reward."

Mary's initial reward must have felt like a fist slammed into her stomach. She'd sat with the Master's disciples many times, sharing His words and bathing in His wisdom. She considered them her friends. She knew each of them well: robust Peter, humble Matthew, fiery James, sophisticated Judas. Yet, as she bathed Jesus' feet with her tears, she could feel their censure. She could hear their grumblings. Her natural reaction must have been to wither into a piece of lint on the floor.

Their censure simmered and seethed until it could be contained no longer. They couldn't attack Jesus directly, but they could attack Mary. The suave, brooding Judas, a man who would be noted in the new kingdom, found "righteous" words with which to attack her. "That's criminal! A sheer waste! The perfume could have been sold for well over a year's wages and used to benefit the poor."

Criticism from strangers stings. Condemnation from one's peers hurts. An injury inflicted by a close friend or a family member leaves painful scars. The wound most difficult to heal is the one inflicted by a brother or sister in Christ, for it is a wound of the spirit. The body heals quickly, but the spirit takes much longer.

Feel Mary's pain:
Remember
The poison pens,
The tart tongues,
The insulting innuendoes
From a brother or sister in Christ.
Sense Mary's distress:
Remember
The mortifying moment,
The crushing criticism,
The humiliation
From the accuser of the brethren.

When we become siblings-in-Christ, we become vulnerable to the assaults of our weaker brother or sister.

And when they attack, they take the side of the original accuser of the brethren—Satan, the father of darkness and lies. Justified or contrived, it always stings. It always inflicts pain. Jesus taught, "Love one another as I have loved you" (John 13:34, KJV). Will we ever learn?

Unfortunately, for Mary, the disciples hadn't. One of them never would. In a few days, Judas would sell his Saviour to the highest bidder, the council of the priests and Pharisees.

But Mary didn't know the future of her accuser as she knelt quivering at Jesus' feet. She did know that one of the Saviour's leading disciples had openly criticized her act of love. Would her Saviour agree with Judas and the other disapproving disciples? She waited as she had waited on the fateful day on the steps of the synagogue for the Lord's verdict. She must have questioned her impulsive judgment. "Perhaps, Judas is right. He's a wise man, a financier, in fact. Perhaps, I shouldn't have been so extravagant."

She looked to Jesus, her heart in her eyes. This Man had pardoned her sins. He had called forth her beloved brother from the grave. Her heart was filled with gratitude. She had heard Jesus speak of His approaching death, and in her deep love and sorrow, she had longed to honor Him.

With so many people saying Jesus would be crowned king, her grief turned to joy. Eager to be the first to honor Him, she feared she'd stepped out of line again.

What would Martha say? And Lazarus? Worse yet, what would the Master say?

Trembling with embarrassment and fear, she turned to slink away, when she heard the voice of the Lord.

"Why are you giving this woman a hard time? She has done something wonderfully significant for Me. You will have the poor with you everyday for the rest of your lives, but not Me."

Jesus' matter-of-fact statement was indeed prophecy. Whether by war, famine, or greed, the existence of the world's poor spans the centuries. There would always be someone in need, someone for God's children to help with their love and generosity.

One of the most exciting exercises for the child of God is learning to give joyfully. Joyful giving is more than seeing a need and easing it. Learning to recognize the voice of the Holy Spirit and responding to it, the giver never needs to worry that the money might not be used correctly. She's already received the biggest reward of generosity, being in closer tune with the Holy Spirit. If the receiver of the gift wastes it, that's his problem, not the problem of the giver.

Some Far Eastern religions and many advocates of the New Age movement believe that when you give money to a poor person, you mess with his or her "Karma." They believe that the indigent was reincarnated into that state in order to learn from past mistakes and become a better person—more like themselves, of course. By easing the suffering, you prolong his or her existence in the negative state. What a brilliant way for the selfish persons to justify their greed!

Jesus wasn't justifying this kind of thinking. He wasn't saying, "Don't give to the poor." On the contrary, His heart and His message reached out to the poor. He said, "Blessed are the poor in spirit, for their's is the kingdom of heaven" (Matthew 5:3, KJV).

Imagine that? Happy are the poor in spirit!

I've always thought that being poor in spirit meant to be spiritless, at the end of one's rope. Recently, I heard a different interpretation worth considering. The preacher said that Jesus was complimenting the poor for their generosity with one another. For example, if I have only a kettle of beans and you only have a pot of rice, if we share with one another, we'll both enjoy a better meal. This was the attitude of the Judean poor. In many cases, sharing was survival.

I remember my parents talking about the Great Depression. For a time, they lived on black coffee and potatoes. A neighbor up the road might bring in a crop of carrots, while another might forage the woods for spring leeks. By pooling the resources, they had a feast! Thus began the tradition of leek suppers in the northwest corner of Pennsylvania.

When Jesus complimented the poor for their generous spirit, He gave us a glimpse of His kingdom—a kingdom of spirit, not earthly goods and territory. Today, He wants me to live in this Spirit kingdom of generosity.

It was Judas' place to voice the disciples' complaint. Judas handled the money, allotting it as necessary so there would be money to give to the poor. The Lord didn't miss the slur against Him for not reprimanding Mary for her waste. As He had done with Martha's complaint earlier, He ignored it.

The Lord didn't scold Judas for skimming off the top of the group's cash, for being an embezzler. The Lord knew, but He didn't humiliate Judas in front of the banquet guests as Judas humiliated Mary. But Judas knew the Saviour read his deceit and he, like the pharaohs of ancient Egypt, hardened his heart. And when he betrayed his Lord to the cabal of rulers, he sold Jesus for a sum far less than the cost of Mary's ointment.

Instead of treating Judas in the same manner as Judas had treated Mary, Jesus gave His deaf and blind disciples a glimpse into their futures. He said, "When she poured this perfume on my body, what she really did was anoint me for burial."

Mary must have buried her face in her lap at this announcement. Rocking back and forth in agony, her tears flowed. She'd been right, terribly right. Her Lord would not become an earthly king. He would soon die.

"You can be sure," the Lord predicted, "wherever in the whole world the message is preached, what she did is going to be remembered and admired."

And it has been. It has been remembered as:

Outrageous.

Preposterous.

Shameless.

Brazen.

Extravagant.

Incredible.

An indelible sacrifice!

The Judases of the congregation will always click their tongues at exhibitionistic demonstrations of pure love and gratitude. And there will always be disciples who have not yet caught Mary's spirit of unrestrained love toward their Saviour. But, praise God, there will always be Marys who unabashedly pour out their love on the Saviour's feet, those who are so grateful for His salvation they can't constrain themselves.

# CHAPTER NINETEEN

# "BUT THAT WOMAN, LORD"

*"If this man were a prophet, he would know who is touching him and what kind of woman she is"*
(Luke 7:39, NIV).

The Gospels of Matthew and Mark record that Mary anointed the Saviour's head with the perfume, while John and Luke say she anointed His feet. Mary's actions may seem bizarre to women approaching the twenty-first century, but they were commonplace for her day. I've heard theologians tell that a wife in Christ's time performed this ritual for her husband daily. She anointed the head of her husband with oil and washed his feet as an act of humility.

In good taste, Simon, as the host, should have arranged to have a female servant at least wash the feet of Jesus when He first arrived. In spite of Simon's social faux pas, I can understand his censure of Mary's carrying out the duty of a wife. Simon considered himself a "righteous" man. No wonder he questioned how the Messiah—if He was indeed the Messiah—could allow a woman of Mary's morals to perform such an intimate act.

He watched Mary caress the feet of his Guest. He saw her fingers slowly and lovingly anoint the Teacher's feet, soothing away His weariness. And Simon thought, *How brazen of her to unbind her hair in public! To let it flow in all its beauty down around her shoulders and onto His feet.*

In Simon's mind, Mary's behavior cast aspersion on each of the decent men in the room, of which he considered himself to be foremost. The fact that he'd led Mary into sin in the first place was ancient history as far as he was concerned. Boys will be boys, you know.

While Judas voiced his disapproval aloud, Simon said to himself, " 'If this man was the prophet I thought he was, he would have known what kind of woman this is who is falling all over him' " (Luke 7:39, *The Message*).

But Jesus heard Simon's thoughts as clearly as He heard Judas' utterances. Good taste at not voicing them didn't lessen their ridicule. As host, Simon knew it was his job to get rid of the woman and rescue his feast from the scorn of his more important guests. But, how to go about that was a problem in itself.

Mary didn't need to lift her gaze toward Simon to know his thoughts. She already knew. She'd seen it all before. Men like Simon seldom keep such criticism silent, especially when building a smoke screen to cover their own behavior. Oh, he had been honey and roses in her bed, but in public, his gaze revealed his true scorn for her and for her Lord. More than the judgment of her peers, Simon's aspersions on the innocence of Jesus hurt Mary more.

Then Jesus said, "Simon, I have something to tell you." And He launched into one of His parables. "Two men were in debt to a banker. One owed five hundred silver pieces, the other fifty. Neither of them could pay up, and so the banker canceled both debts. Which of the two would be more grateful?"

Simon replied, "I suppose the one who was forgiven the most."

"That's right." Turning to Mary while yet addressing Simon, Jesus said, "Do you see this woman? I came to your home; you provided no water for my feet, but she rained tears on my feet and dried them with her hair. You gave me no greeting, but from the time I arrived she hasn't quit kissing my feet. You provided nothing for freshening up, but she has soothed my feet with her perfume. Impressive, isn't it?"

Imagine, for a moment, ministering directly to God: cooling His hot, dusty feet, refreshing His tired body. What a privilege! What an honor! I would jump at the chance, right?

Maybe Yes, maybe No. Without my twenty-twenty hindsight, who knows what I would do? Mary risked the disfavor of her peers without knowing of the positive outcome.

Like Mary, I can also minister to God in a very concrete way. Not by pouring perfume on the Saviour's feet. But I minister to Him whenever I worship at the altar of grace.

Imagine! The fragrance of my praise and thanksgiving wafts heavenward to God's nostrils. He pauses and sniffs. "Hmm, what is that aroma I smell? Why, it's my daughter, Kay, praising Me, her Father." A smile fills His face, the smile of a proud Parent. Then the God of the universe calls to Gabriel and his winged cohorts.

"Look, look, that's My kid! She's praising me." Tears of joy fill the Father's eyes, and He begins to "rejoice over His child with singing." (See Zephaniah 3:17, NIV.)

Jesus waited a moment for His message of praise to sink into the minds of His audience. Simon heard the Saviour's words and understood the Lord's compassion in not publically revealing His host's sins. Then Jesus continued. "She was forgiven many, many sins, and so she is very, very grateful. If the forgiveness is minimal, the gratitude is minimal" (Luke 7:47, *The Message*).

"She loved much" (NIV). I wonder if one or more of the more boorish guests snickered at the Lord's pronouncement, "She loved much." The snide innuendo would not have been missed for many present. Every gathering has within it the elements of ribaldry. Turning the sacred into the commonplace, the spiritual into the obscene. But the snickering doesn't last. Jesus arrests the crude with a glance that tells all and reveals all.

In the look that passed between Jesus and His host, Simon knew Jesus knew everything. The past with Mary. Simon's attitude toward Mary. Simon's attitude toward Jesus. Everything.

Before the Saviour, a death sentence hung over the heads of both Simon and Mary. Simon would die from his leprosy; Mary's life of prostitution carried with it the sentence of death as well. Both diseases were obvious to the world and were obvious sins, from the world's perspective. Both had been healed. Neither had room for pride.

Simon's arrogance prevented him from treating the King of the universe with the proper courtesy and respect due a guest in his home. While he wanted to make a display of his gratitude, Simon couldn't bring himself to accept this Nazarene and His ragtag crew as equals. Tolerate, yes, but not accept. Then to add fuel to Simon's fellow Pharisees' fury, Jesus turned to Mary. I see Him cupping her tear-stained face in His gentle hands, saying, "Your sins are forgiven."

Once again, Mary is face to face with forgiveness.

And the nay-sayers began.

"Your sins are forgiven? Did He say her sins are forgiven?"

"Forgiven? Who is He to forgive anyone's sins?"

"Forgiven? Can He do that?"

"Forgiven? He can't do that!"

"Forgiven!" Mary's heart leapt for joy. She gazed lovingly into His eyes. He smiled, gently lifting her to her feet.

"Your faith has saved you. Go in peace."

# FACE TO FACE WITH FORGIVENESS

## Section
# 5

# Mary, the Celebrant

# CHAPTER TWENTY

# RIDING THE CREST

*"Rejoice greatly, O Daughter of Zion!*
*Shout, Daughter of Jerusalem!*
*See, your king comes to you, righteous and having*
*salvation, gentle and riding on a donkey"*
(Zechariah 9:9, NIV).

How well I remember the day the mail carrier delivered the envelope containing my first book sale. I'd worked on my mother-in-law's life story and conversion for several months. Since I was teaching high school English at the time—which involved correcting mountains of student essays—I had to wait for weekends and vacations to work on the manuscript. And hopefully, in the process, I wouldn't slight my husband and two daughters. After months of painful revisions, I printed what I hoped would be the final manuscript revision and mailed it to the publisher.

Several weeks later, a letter arrived. The family gathered around as I read it aloud. "The book committee has studied your manuscript, *Someone to Love You*, and we have decided to publish your book." All four of us screamed, in barbershop harmony! The roof lifted six inches off the frame of the house. The cat ran for cover while the dog barked around our feet. We danced, hugged, shouted, laughed, and cried.

"This calls for a celebration!" Richard shouted, breaking open a bottle of Martinelli's sparkling grape juice, a tradition we've continued with each subsequent book sale. Our celebration spilled over into our favorite Mexican restaurant. The music from their live Mariachi band complimented our dizzying joy and uncontainable gratitude.

Celebration. We celebrate momentous occasions—birthdays, weddings, graduations, holidays—and any other excuse from the simple to the sublime. The Jews loved their celebrations, as well. From the Passover to Pentecost and the Feast of Tabernacles, to the other less significant holidays, the Jewish year revolved around their celebrations.

These feasts could be quite elaborate affairs. The Feast of Tabernacles involved a seven-day banquet in which the Israelites were commanded to rejoice. Jesus enjoyed feasts and celebrations too. Look at how often in scripture He could be found dining with friends, attending weddings and talking about banquets on this earth and on the earth to come.

The Savior's partying irked the Pharisees. When they voiced their complaint, Jesus said, " 'We played the flute for you, and you did not dance; we sang a dirge and you did not cry.' For John the Baptist came neither eating bread or drinking wine and you say, 'He has a demon.' The Son of Man came eating and drinking, and you say, 'Here is a glutton and a drunkard, a friend of tax collectors and sinners.' "

Throughout history, the Jewish people enjoyed the spontaneous celebration. Remember the story of David dancing before the ark of the covenant? When his wife nagged him for being so undignified, David answered, "The Lord chose me and in response, I will celebrate and be even more undignified than this."

David and his musicians played their instruments and sang before God with all their might, with cymbals, trumpets, tambourines, harps and voices. Later, Paul and Silas not only made the rafters ring, but their praises set off an earthquake that shook the prison right down to its foundation. Paul would exhort the Ephesians to worship with the use of psalms, hymns and spiritual songs.

But the celebration that Sunday morning on the Mount of Olives dimmed all organized and spontaneous celebrations held to that point in history.

Zechariah prophesied the celebration five hundred years before its time. He said "the daughters of Zion would sing, shout and rejoice for the coming King, riding on the back of a donkey" (see Zechariah 9:9). On that celebration Sunday, Mary became one of Zion's daughters who would fulfill the ancient prophecy.

Go with me to Bethany that Sunday afternoon. The crowds gather outside Lazarus' courtyard, hoping for a glimpse of the resurrected one and the Miracle Man. Pockets of people lounge on the grass, perch on rocks, sit on the roadside, anywhere where there is space. They come from all over the region, including Jerusalem. And they wait.

Many traveled to Jerusalem for the Passover feast.

# FACE TO FACE WITH FORGIVENESS

Upon arriving in the holy city, they began hearing the tales of blind eyes opened, deaf ears unstopped, of leprosy cured, and now a man called Lazarus being raised from the dead. The scuttlebutt skittering from person to person was "Jesus of Nazareth is ready to announce His kingdom!" The people, hungering for freedom from Rome's iron hand, could taste the victory. They could sniff the aroma of freedom. They longed to cheer the last Roman guard's leather sole fleeing to the waiting ships, ships that would transport the enemy out of the Jewish kingdom forever.

Come with me as I help Martha and Mary hastily pack a picnic supper for their guests and for themselves. Grab your cloak and your purse as Jesus prepares to leave. We don't want to miss one moment of this exciting day with Jesus. Hear Jesus deploy two of His disciples to Jerusalem. Why? To learn if it's safe for the Messiah to enter the city?

Will He finally announce His kingdom? Like Mary, we can't help but wonder. With all He said about dying, about a kernel of corn falling to the ground, or destroying the temple and in three days raising it up again, we can't hold back the growing hope that this is the day of His kingdom!

Our thoughts tumble around in our minds as we maneuver our way through the crowd to be as close to Jesus as possible. The throng of people grow with each turn in the road. The outcasts of society rally around Him—their hero. There are those in the crowd who've been healed of debilitating diseases. Others join for the excitement. Still others spy for the cabal of priests in Jerusalem. Little children run alongside, skipping and laughing in the brilliant sunshine.

## Riding the Crest

The horde reaches the crest of the Mount of Olives where the Master pauses. Mary and I stop and inhale the delicate fragrances of blossoming trees and shrubbery. A new life and joy invigorates us. All nature seems to rejoice with us. We gaze east to the Dead Sea, sparkling in the late afternoon sunlight. Turning our faces toward the west, we inhale the beauty of the expansive Kidron Valley. Cattle graze in the verdant fields. Sheep dot the hillsides. Beyond the valley, the walls of Jerusalem and Solomon's porch rise out of the soil. We smile and nod to one another. What a beautiful city, fit for a king. And what a beautiful day for a coronation.

The moment Jesus sits down on a rock to rest, the little children run to Him, clamoring to sit on His lap.

"Look, Jesus, I made you a daisy chain." The tiny girl stretches her arms to drop the lei over His head. He dips His head, then thanks the child for her gift, planting a kiss on her ruddy cheek. She giggles and slips under the crook of His free arm.

"Tell us a story," an older child cries.

"Yes, tell us a story," the other children echo.

He tousles an eight-year-old's hair and begins, "The kingdom of heaven is like unto. . ."

"Master?" Peter sidles up to Jesus. "The men are back with the donkey you requested." Excitement radiates from the disciple's eyes and his smile.

"Oh. Wonderful. Then it's time."

"It's time, Master?" Thomas asks, uncertain he heard correctly. Even Judas, who has already made arrangements with the Pharisees to betray his Master, rises to his feet and places his cloak on the animal's back.

Martha points down the slope. "Didn't the prophet

Zechariah prophecy that the Messiah would come riding on a donkey?"

"Yes, I'm sure he did." Mary turns to me. "You see, it's Jewish custom since the days of the earliest kings to make a royal entry into Jerusalem."

"And the donkey?" I ask.

"Oh, that's a part of the custom as well," Mary assures me. She cranes her neck around the suddenly impatient crowd. "Do you really think this is the moment He'll . . ." Her voice breaks, too filled with emotion to continue. As Jesus mounts the beast, a roar of approval erupts from the people.

"What else could it be, child?" Martha impatiently urges her forward. "Look, Lazarus has been chosen to lead the animal. Imagine, our brother chosen for such a task!"

"Make way! Make way!" Lazarus shouts. The disciples join, shouting, "Make way for the King of Israel!"

A cheer goes up from a former deaf-mute. A second "hallelujah" bursts from the lungs of an ex-cancer victim. A healed paraplegic leaps into the air, shouting and crying, "Jesus is King. "Hosanna! Praise God!"

A recovered leper rips his coat from his own back and spreads it on the ground before the donkey. "My Master! My King!" Other's join him, casting their robes before the donkey's tiny hooves.

Shouts of victory split the air. Thunderous praise echoes down the canyons and rivulets of Mount Olivet.

"Hosanna!"

"Hallelujah!"

"Praise God!"

"He is the mighty King of Israel!"

"Blessed is He who comes in God's name!"

The cheers bounce off the mountains and across the valley, echoing off Jerusalem's walls. The children strip the young palms of their lowest branches and wave the boughs before Jesus as the donkey slowly makes his way down the narrow road. They dance. They sing psalms of victory. The formerly deaf and dumb sing the loudest. The cured lame dance most vigorously. Those freed from demons shout, "He is the King of kings!" King David's celebration party had nothing on this celebration.

Partway down the mountain, a crowd of people from Jerusalem who'd heard about the excitement meets them waving palm branches and shouting, "Behold our King! Jesus of Nazareth is our King."

Their voices join with the throng who'd come down the mountain with Jesus, their praises swelling to a crescendo of joy. A spectator asks, "Who is this?"

"Jesus, Jesus of Nazareth," Mary answers. A shout of triumph drowns out her words. Again and again the shout is repeated through the eager throng. I glance toward Mary. Her face is glowing with a joy I've never seen before.

More celebrants join us until we number more than a thousand. In the distance, we hear the trumpet announcing the evening service. Mary looks to me and mouths, "They're going to have an empty temple tonight."

I nod in agreement. "I've never seen anything like it. I'll remember this day for the rest of my life."

Mary nods. "Look over there." I turn my gaze from Jesus to a huddle of glowering Pharisees. A few of the splendid-robed leaders wave their hands in the air and shout, "Be quiet! I order you all to cease this behavior! You're breaking the law!" Others wring their hands, nervously searching the crowd for signs of Roman soldiers who might report this demonstration to Pilate. But the people didn't stop praising even long enough to glance their way.

"That's not good," Mary whispers in my ear.

"What can they do," I ask, "with all these people on His side? They'd be mobbed if they tried to arrest Him or something."

Mary clicks her tongue. "I don't know, but sooner or later, they're going to try something."

"Uh-ho, there's trouble." We watch nervously as several of the Pharisees stroll over to Jesus. One reaches out and pulls on the animal's reigns to make it stop. The Pharisee of rank puffs out his chest and in a deep authoritative voice booms. "Rabbi, rebuke your disciples! Make them be quiet!"

The Master throws back His head and laughs at their suggestion. "If I did that," He points to the side of the road, "those rocks over there would cry out!"

# CHAPTER TWENTY-ONE

# A TIME TO REJOICE

*" 'If they keep quiet, the stones with cry out' "*
(Luke 19:40, NIV).

Imagine, rocks shouting the news of the coming King! I love it! When Jesus takes us home as His trophies, will the shouts of heaven's rocks be heard above the din of celebrating angels and saints?

Whenever I think of the rocks crying out, I remember reading about the singing sands of Eigg, an island off the coast of Scotland. How I'd love to visit the beaches there, where the sand, a unique quartz crystal, makes musical notes according to the pressure and the temperature. What fun I'd have combining the sand in different amounts, creating a symphony of praise to my God.

If our Creator made such a place for us to enjoy here on this earth, imagine the possibilities that will be ours in heaven. He could have an entire planet where one day, Beethoven could conduct his latest, "Ode to Joy Perfected," and Handel perform his "Messiah II" and Kay Rizzo (?!) sing her own arrangement of "I Love You, Lord," accompanied by the crystal sands of eternity.

In the meantime, I'm instructed to "Rejoice greatly, O daughter of Zion; shout, O daughter of Jerusalem" (Zech. 9:9, KJV). Did you ever wonder why, on the one triumphal scene in Jesus' earthly life, when the Saviour might have employed the escort of heavenly angels, when He could have been heralded by the trump of God, He depended on the ovation of man? And if they failed Him, stones? He had the entire universe at His fingertips to command. The Lord of Creation had a good reason for using the voices of humble peasants, His friends, and His followers.

Psalm 148 tells us that all nature praises God. The beasts of the ocean praise Him. The stars of heaven give Him praise. The wind, the rain, and the snowflake all joyfully praise their Maker.

> "Let them praise the name of the Lord,
> for his name alone is exalted;
> his splendor is above the earth and the heavens.
> He has raise up for his people a horn [power],
> the praise of all his saints,
> of Israel, the people close to his heart" (Psalm 148:13, 14, NIV).

However, we, as the ones who truly love Him, sing the sweetest praise to our Lord. David says that we, the people closest to His heart, praise Him not for what He has done—as incredible as that may be—but for who He is: The Great I Am! Lord, Jehovah, Mighty to save!

If we who love Him do not sing His praises, who will?

Jesus told the Pharisees "The rocks would cry out."

The act of praise reminds us that we have so much for which to be thankful. And every time we thank Him, we align our wills with the will of God. In 1 Thessalonians 5:18, it says, " give thanks in all circumstances, for this is God's will for you in Christ Jesus" (NIV).

Even our best praises will be far less than He deserves. Praise is not an obligation but a privilege of the chosen ones. God commands us to praise Him not because His ego needs the attention, but because we need to praise if we wish to grow spiritually. "The joy of the Lord is my strength," the psalmist said. Praise leads to joy which is the solid rock virtue that leads to spiritual strength.

Little children know how to praise and how to celebrate. Maybe that's why Jesus said we must become as little children. Have you ever seen the eyes of a five-year-old holding her first seeded dandelion? Or an infant when he first discovers his toes? That's joy. That's celebration of life. That's unconscious praise.

Praising God is part of the process for adults to become as little children. Adults need to abandon their solemner-than-thou attitudes to praise. Talking about a praise-filled worship makes many Christians uncomfortable. Wagging fingers and tongues warn, "Such praising may get out of hand." But that's what Jesus did when He was here. He went around doing the will of God and making the religious uncomfortable.

If Jesus wore the prunelike face many would have us believe, children would have shied away from Him. Society's outcast would have feared His censure. He wouldn't have been the guest-of-honor at so many dinner parties.

# FACE TO FACE WITH FORGIVENESS

As a hostess, I wouldn't wish to invite a sad sack—a person whose countenance drags in my gravy bowl—to my dinner party. No, I invite guests into my home who are upbeat and who have something to contribute to the mood of the evening. Jesus was that kind of guest. His joy made Him the "life of the party" wherever He went.

I heard a youth preacher once say, "When you invite Satan to your party, it will go downhill from there on out. But if you invite Jesus to your party, it will keep getting better and better and better."

I like that. It fits everything I've learned about Him. Yes, He was a man of sorrows. Yes, He knew all about grief. But the same Son of God who cried tears of blood in the garden also inspired Solomon to write:

> "To every thing there is a season, and a time
> to every purpose under the heaven:
> A time to be born and a time to die . . .
> A time to weep, and a time to laugh;
> A time to mourn, and a time to dance"
> (Ecclesiastes 3: 1, 2, 4, KJV).

Jesus lived a life that modeled God, the Father. Psalm 2:4 describes God as laughing. Zephaniah 3:17 shows Him rejoicing. Singing. Bragging, even. In fact, when a friend's wedding occurred, Jesus was there enjoying the singing, the dancing, and the abundant flow of the fruit of the vine. (See John 2:1-11.) For seven days!

The daily life of the country poor was hard. Wedding feasts were the greatest events in their lives. All work stopped. They ate choice food and drank their finest wine or juice for a solid week. Imagine footing the bill for that reception, all you fathers-of-the-bride! This was the only time men, women, and children could freely intermingle.

When Jesus announced that the kingdom of God was like a wedding feast, He must have smiled with joy at the delighted faces surrounding Him. He knew that to possess the kingdom of God, an inner joy of the Spirit would need to replace their external expressions of religion and its obligations. This is what He wanted for His disciples. This was the truth that would set them free.

When He tweaked the noses of His disciples by having them serve the fish and the bread to the multitude—clearly women's work—and when He said, "Let the little children come be with me," His goal wasn't so much to liberate women in their minds, but to liberate men, liberate them to see the joy in His salvation.

Jesus knew that the men of His day needed to experience the world of love and service much more than women needed to have a part of the world of power and prestige.

On the day of His triumphal entry, age and position meant nothing. Grown men and women sang and waved branches, heavily-burdened fishermen danced in the streets. Little girls twirled with abandon and young boys leapt for joy. Only the Pharisees worried about how it might look to outsiders—how it might look to the Romans.

# CHAPTER TWENTY-TWO

# FOR THOSE TEARS

*"As he approached Jerusalem and saw the city, he wept over it"*
(Luke 19:41, NIV).

Tears of the heart.

Jesus looks out over the valley to the city in the distance. The crowd hushes, struck by the beauty of the walls glowing in the golden light of the setting sun. They turn toward Jesus expecting His face to reflect the admiration they felt for their capital city. Instead, His smile has faded. His eyes are filled with tears of anguish, not tears of joy. An agonizing cry shocks them all.

"Oh, Jerusalem, if you had only known today what would bring you peace." The Saviour cried tears of the heart for a faithless and lost people whom He longed to save.

Mary responds in kind with tears, tears she doesn't understand. She cries because her Jesus is crying.

Have you ever cried tears of the heart? The kind of tears that come when you drive by a cemetery and see mourners gathered around an open grave? Or you see a homeless man digging in a restaurant's garbage can? Or a young teenage girl standing on a street corner in the middle of the night advertising her "wares?" Do you cry tears of the heart when you see the children of war-torn Bosnia on the evening news? Or the face of a missing child on a milk carton? Or an Alzheimer patient wandering in a fog of confusion?

These are tears of the heart. Your heart reaches out to the lost and the hurting, not because you understand their pain, but because your Lord shed tears for them. When the One you love cries, you cry; regardless of the reason.

Tears of truth.

Mary's tears change from tears of the heart to tears of truth. She listens in horror as the Master predicts the fall and destruction of her beautiful city. "Not one stone left on another?" She shakes her head, unable to imagine such destruction. Tears fill Mary's eyes as she visualizes Jerusalem destroyed. Surely not God's city.

Mary looks to Jesus. Finally she understands His tears, and she weeps over that understanding. The Saviour heaves a deep sigh then signals for Lazarus to resume the procession. With the entourage in motion, the hosannas resume as well, growing louder as more people join in the joyous procession approaching the city's gates.

The mood swing resembles the mood change at the start of an army-navy game. The pulsating rhythm of excitement fills the stadium before a game. The noise; the ribbing between old-time rivals; the hawkers selling pennants, popcorn, and hot dogs; all part of the rush. Then over the intercom, someone announces "The Star-

Spangled Banner."

A hush settles over the crowd and the players as the first notes come over the intercom. "Oh, say can you see, by the dawn's early light . . ." All eyes turn to the colors waving high above the ballpark—red, white, and blue. Eyes mist for fallen comrades remembered and for those still serving in dangerous places.

". . . the land of the free, and the home of the brave." As the last notes fade, the crowd returns to celebrating. The hawkers hawk their wares. The players run onto the field to the cheers of their fans.

Tears of anticipation.

Mary's eyes glisten with tears of anticipation as the procession nears the city gates. The tourists in town for the Passover feast pour out of the city to see what all the excitement is about. A prosperous stranger asks, "What's going on?"

A soldier from the Roman guard barks, "Who is this man?"

Mary's heart soars. She can feel her excitement deep in her stomach. She turns toward the disciples, toward Peter.

"Who is this man?" Peter repeats the question, shouting over the din of the crowd. "If you ask Abraham, he will tell you that this is Melchizedek, King of Salem, King of Peace."

John follows. "Jacob will tell you, He is Shiloh of the tribe of Judah."

Like an antiphonal choir, the excitement builds as the disciples echo His praises back and forth over the heads of the crowd.

Philip calls out, "Isaiah will tell you that He's

Immanuel, Wonderful, Counselor, the Mighty God, the everlasting Father, the Prince of Peace."

Andrew adds, "John the Baptist will tell you He is the 'lamb of God,' who takes away the sin of the world."

In eloquent strains, Matthew sings, "The great Jehovah said, 'This is My beloved Son.'"

"Even the prince of darkness acknowledges Him as the Holy One," Bartholemew shouts in defiance.

James joins the impromptu voice choir by asking the question once more. "Who is this Man?"

Tears of anticipation glisten in Mary's eyes as she adds her voice to the voices of His other disciples. "This is Jesus, the Messiah, the Prince of life, the Redeemer of the world." All thoughts of the Lord's imminent death fade from Mary's mind as she gets caught up in the rapture of the moment.

Caught up in the moment—a dangerous concept for the self-proclaimed "intellectual" Christian. To lose control of one's emotions, even for a moment, terrifies the person who lives by strength of mind and denies his or her heart. The same intellectual beings who will attend a ballgame and scream, shout, jump up and down, and throw their baseball caps into the air will become disgusted at their brother and condescending to their sister for weeping, shouting amens, and praising the Saviour during a worship service.

"Made in the image of God" includes mind, body, and spirit. We miss out on a portion of God's character when we deny anyone of the three facets of our created beings. The same is true for the emotion-prone individuals who live by their emotions and never take the time to strengthen the spiritual intellect. And for the

Christian who is so busy "doing," like Martha, that the spirit and the mind atrophy. God doesn't seek obedient but dispassionate servants. He seeks instead a passionate love that is so strong it burns all other bonds.

Emotionalism—the displaying of emotions for emotion's sake—can lead the Christian to seek the thrill of emotion, the adrenaline charge, instead of seeking the will of God through Bible study and prayer. But God-inspired emotions come when we grasp some insight into who God is.

In my personal study, when I discover a new aspect of my Saviour and His love for me, my emotions overflow. I make no apologies—I weep. Whenever I read a text or hear a song about Jesus' return, I cry tears of joy. I can be in a grocery store, driving down the freeway, sitting in a church pew, or wherever I am, my soul stands and shouts, "Hallelujah! Praise the Lord," even when my body can't. When I sit on my "prayer swing" and gaze up at the stars in the night sky, I mingle my tears with joyful singing.

A friend of mine pointed out that "Showing one's emotions is a personality thing. Some people weep easier than others." And she's probably right, to a point. Differing cultures give some people permission to show emotion while denying it to others. This fact must be taken into consideration. Tears come naturally for some and not for others. The Marys of this world seem to have built-in "feelers" that are more delicately tuned than others'.

Yet, a relationship with Jesus Christ works from the inside out. Robert Goulet, the famous Broadway singer, discovered Jesus as His Saviour a few years back. In a television interview on TBN's "Praise the Lord", he said, "I never cried when I was growing up, until I met Jesus Christ. Now, I cry on the drop of a handkerchief."

Chuck Colson, the tough, no-nonsense mastermind of the Nixon-Watergate affair, tells in his book *Born Again* that he sheds tears often since he gave his life to Christ. (Old Tappan, N.J.: Chosen Books, 1967) 116.

Does this mean that the Christian who cannot shed tears or allow his emotions to show does not love his Saviour? No, of course not. But it does mean that he or she must beware the temptation to point a finger and say, "That's an empty, touchy-feely counterfeit of true Christianity."

Only the Father reads the heart. Only the Bridegroom knows His bride. Deuteronomy 6:5 says, "Love the Lord your God with all your heart and with all your soul and with all your strength" (NIV). The Marys of this world are not satisfied to experience God's love drop by drop. They long to "bathe" in the ocean of His love.

Christianity is about intimacy with the Father. My obedience, my witness, my knowledge of Him all develop because of my desire for such a relationship. We have no idea of the immense love God has for us. God feels our rejection so strongly that He compares it to the betrayal of adultery. He doesn't need us; He chooses to need us in a sense that He feels our rejection and our passion intimately.

Regardless of Mary's condition before she met Jesus, regardless of how hard her heart had become, regardless of the steel doors she built around her soul, when she met the Saviour, her tears began to flow. It was as if the Lord turned on a faucet and all those years of pent-

up emotions poured out a steady stream of tears.
Tears of joy,
tears of sorrow,
tears of laughter,
tears of remorse,
tears of anticipation,
tears of concern,
tears of pain,
tears of healing.

Regardless of the condition of your heart, an intimate meeting with Jesus offers the same release to you.

# CHAPTER TWENTY-THREE

# RISK-TAKERS

*"Jesus' mother, his aunt, Mary the wife of Clopas,
and Mary Magdalene stood at the foot of the cross"*
(John 19:25, *The Message*).

Risk-takers: Navy Seals, Indy 500 race-car drivers, Evil Knieval wanna-bes, sword swallowers, antidrug SWAT teams, Stock Marketeers, bungee-jumpers, astronauts, and sky-divers. Yes, those are the people I think of as risk-takers.

Jumping from a plane high above the Mojave Desert and betting my life on a thin sheet of nylon—that's risk-taking. Diving into enemy waters to dismember highly explosive mines—that's risk-taking. Bursting into a suspected drug lab knowing I will be facing a barrage of AK-47s—that's risk-taking. Even leaping a gorge on a motorcycle for the publicity or bungee-jumping off a bridge for the thrill—that's risk-taking.

Mary's presence outside Herod's palace, beyond the walls of Pilate's hall of justice, on the via dolorosa, and at Calvary—that was extreme risk-taking. She did not try to hide her loyalties. She didn't pretend not to know the Revolutionary. She did not camouflage her devotion before the Roman eyes. Mary displayed heroic devotion.

Mary stood by when Peter denied His Lord. Mary stood firm when James and Philip decided it was time to be somewhere else. Mary stood resolved when all the other disciples fled the scene.

> When she saw blood dripping from Jesus' head,
> she wanted to rush forward and mop His brow.
> Yet, all she could do was stand by and watch.
> When she saw the vicious stripes upon His back,
> she longed to soothe His pain with oil and aloes.
> Yet, all she could do was stand by and wait.
> When she saw Him fall under the weight of the
>     cross,
> she ached to lift it from His shoulders.
> But, alas, all she could do was stand by and be a
>     witness.

In the ancient world, the fact that Christianity owed its beginnings to the witness of women would be a difficult message to proclaim. In the Jewish world of Jesus' time, the witness of women was not admitted in any court of law.

Matthew noted, "Then all the disciples forsook Him and fled" (Matthew 25:56, NKJV). The early Christian church would find it very embarrassing that all Jesus' male disciples ran off when Jesus was arrested. Only the women remained to witness the crucial events in Jesus' life: His arrest, His death, His burial, and His resurrection. Luke omits the flight of Jesus' male disciples.

Mark says, "All His acquaintances . . ." (Mark 14:50).

Mary and the other women followed Jesus and ministered to His needs long before that fateful day on Calvary. Being a camp follower, or a "groupie," as we would call them today, broke all the rules of polite Jewish society.

Mark says that these (women), ("when he was in Galilee, followed him, and ministered unto him;) and many other women which came up with him unto Jerusalem" (Mark 15:41, KJV). When the trouble hit, Mary and the other women faithfully did what they'd always done. They remained at the foot of the cross to minister to their Saviour's needs. They risked sharing His life and His fate, even willing to share in His suffering, if need be. They risked ridicule from the temple priests. They risked harassment from the unruly mob. They risked martyrdom at the hands of the Roman guard to stand at the foot of the cross. And what was even more remarkable—they gave no thought to that risk. Their only thoughts were of the needs of their suffering Saviour.

"Let him come down!" The jeering shouted, peppering their laughter with the most base obscenities and profanities. "If he is the Messiah, let him come down!"

Mary's heart must have lurched at such mockery. Did she consider throwing herself at the feet of the Roman centurion and begging, "Let Him come down?"

I can see Mary early in the day running from disciple to disciple, grabbing their lapels and crying, "Do something! Stop them! Surely you can stop them!" only to see in their eyes fear and hopelessness. These were the same men who'd vowed to fight, and if necessary, die for their King, who rallied the people to His side, who talked a good talk, but couldn't walk the walk to Calvary. Bewildered and dejected, all Mary could do was trail along in the bloodstained pathway of her Lord.

At the cross, Mary and the other women stood and watched. No heroics like chopping off a soldier's ear. No histrionics like vowing to die for Him. But no wavering either. Just risking their hearts by supporting the Saviour with their presence.

At times of great tragedy, standing by and doing nothing can be the most difficult and frustrating thing to do. Yet, as with the women at the foot of the cross, it can also be the greatest gift to the one who suffers. Standing by the bedside of a friend dying of AIDS, standing beside a father whose daughter has been raped and murdered, standing watch with the family of a coma patient, standing arm-in-arm with a man falsely convicted of a felony, standing ready to give financial assistance to a young mother abandoned by her husband, that's risk-taking.

To be a risk-taker demands more than experiencing a surface inconvenience. True risk-taking involves risking one's earthly goods, one's soul, and one's entire being. And knowing that you'll never be the same again.

Mary knew, as she stood waiting and watching and praying for a miracle, that she would never be the same again. The scene around her would haunt her forever. Whenever she passed a blacksmith's shop, she would remember the sounds of the cross.

> The clank of the iron-headed mallet,
> Metal against metal,

Metal against human flesh.
The thud of the cross
Dropped into the ground,
Ripping muscles,
Severing tendons,
Wrenching His arms from their sockets.
Flies buzzing around drops of blood,
Thieves screaming,
Jesus moaning,
His mother crying.

Mary stretched her arms heavenward in intense prayer, but her gaze never left Jesus' face. She focused all her strength in that stare, hoping it would bring Him comfort in this desperate hour. But what Mary couldn't see, hear or smell was the cosmic struggle playing out around her.

The prince of darkness hovered near the cross, eagerly waiting for the moment he could begin his celebration of victory. He, too, gazed at the dying Saviour, focusing on Him all His powers of destruction. Jesus and Satan had met only a short time before at the tomb of Lazarus. *Chalk one up for Daddy's Boy*, Satan must have thought, *but this time, I win all the marbles*.

Overhead, black storm clouds gathered. The terrible darkness descended upon Jesus in all its power. Mary heard the screams and curses of the two men being crucified with Jesus. She must have raged at the taunting and ridiculing of the low-life thief.

When Jesus cried, "It is finished," the cosmic struggle ended, or so the demon of destruction thought. The earth shook. A lightning bolt struck the city, releasing divine energy. And the gentle Teacher who loved in the face of hate, who healed rather than destroyed, who forgave and forgave and forgave, died.

Behind her, Mary heard the Roman centurion openly proclaim what she already knew within her heart. "Truly, this was the Son of God."

# CHAPTER TWENTY-FOUR

# WHEN THE PRAISES DIED

*" 'Father, forgive them;*
*they don't know what they're doing' "*
(Luke 23:34, *The Message*).

The miracle of the cross is what *didn't* happen that day on Golgotha's hill. While the Saviour hung in misery, stapled to a wooden tree, the entire universe stood by, ready to leap to the Saviour's defense. Ten thousands times ten thousands of "buff " angels—muscles bulging, wings poised, adrenaline surging through their systems—rumbled on heaven's launching pad waiting for word from heaven's control tower. "Let us go! Let us at 'em," they pleaded over the heavenly sound system.

And with each cry to intercede between the two forces, the prince of darkness threw back his head and laughed. He had 'em where he wanted 'em. "Destroying me won't help; I've won. The 'Old Man' has nowhere to maneuver in this one."

The entire universe would have to admit that he had won. The Father would have to rethink His position on Satan and his mighty imps. *Hmm*, Lucifer must have thought, *now that I have conquered this earth, which planet shall I attack next? Maybe a simple negotiation will suffice.* He giggled. *After all, there is only one Son, and we all know where He is.*

In the midst of old slewfoot's gloating, Jesus spoke. His voice rang clear over the taunts of the crowd and the cursing of the other prisoners. "Father, forgive them, for they know not what they do."

"What?" Satan straightened. "Forgive them?" Forgiveness didn't figure into the evil one's plans. "Forgive them? Ooof!" The devastating fist of forgiveness slammed into Satan's stomach. The blow of defeat sent the devil sprawling on his greatest defect. Satan shook his fist in the Saviour's face. "You can't forgive. You should be hating!"

The Archfiend stomped his foot, cursing and swearing against the God of the universe. Fury poured from his body. The veins in his forehead looked ready to burst. Forgiveness? No! No! No! He hadn't planned on forgiveness.

The father of revenge would never think of forgiving anyone, least of all his enemies. The concept was totally foreign to his being.

If the Son of God could forgive His enemies while hanging on the cross, the entire system of hell would be wrecked. For hell is based on hate, resentment, and the spirit of self-protection. Instead of victory, the cross delivered Satan's greatest defeat.

Suddenly he knew. If he couldn't lead the Christ to sin by this point, there would be no further chances. He'd lost the war. Even as he held the lifeless Son of God in his anteroom to hell, he knew he'd lost the war.

"If there hadn't been a place called Calvary," the Prince of Darkness would later argue, "I would have conquered the world." Oh, he knew there'd be skirmishes for individual souls, but he realized that the heart of the war was over.

Mary wept. She knew that her Lord was dead. She couldn't see her Saviour's victory. She couldn't hear the invisible forces postulating. She couldn't know what God the Father knew—black Friday might be here, but resurrection Sunday was coming. The two are inseparable. The cross is the price Jesus paid for our sins and the resurrection the symbol of our victory.

My daughter Kelli was traveling with the "Celebrant Singers." The seven teams of young people in that group present the message of Jesus Christ at Christian churches—both Protestant and Catholic—all over the world. Married celebrants bring their children along on the concert trail.

The team was setting up for a concert in Ireland one afternoon last summer. The three-year-old daughter of one of the soprano's ran to her mother. "Come, Mama," she cried in an exited voice. "Come see."

The mother allowed her daughter to drag her over to a bigger-than-life-size crucifix with Jesus on it. "See, Mama?" The child pointed to the statue's left hand. "Jesus' hand." The young mother picked up her child so the little girl could get a closer look.

Tenderly, the child ran her fingers over the holes in the statue's hands and the spike that held them in place. "Jesus did this for me, didn't He, Mommy?"

Tears sprang into the mother's eyes as she hugged

her daughter close. "Yes, Erin, Jesus loved you so much He did this for you."

Out of the mouths of babes . . . Here is the deepest, most profound truth known to humankind, yet a child of three can understand. Only a Saviour could make it so simple. Only a God could make it so true. "For God so loved *Erin*, that He gave His only Son, Jesus, that *Erin*, should she believe on Him, would not perish, but live forever" (John 3:16, Rizzo paraphrase).

Hallelujah! Praise the Lord. I can trust Christ's salvation and deliverance from sin because of what didn't happen that day on the cross. Angels were not summoned to retaliate against the forces of darkness. Revenge did not motivate Jesus to strike out at those who mocked Him.

Two spikes burst Satan's victory balloon.

First, Jesus forgave not only the people assembled around the cross, but me as well. A wise old pastor friend of mine once said, "Forgiveness means being face to face with Jesus. We are never closer to Him than when we confess our sins. Forgiveness is why He endured the cross."

Second, He died. His death saved me from dying a permanent death. As the psalmist wrote, "Though I walk through the valley of the shadow of death, I will fear no evil: for thou art with me" (Psalm 23, KJV). The death I may experience here is only a shadow of the real death, the one Jesus suffered for me. Praise God I can safely say, "In Jesus Christ I am saved!"

Salvation became mine two thousand years ago at Calvary.

Satan didn't take Jesus' life. The Lord gave it. When

Jesus commended His spirit to His Father, He did so for you and me. No slimy hands of Satan can ever touch one of God's children who has given over his life to the Father. Even on our deathbed, we can give over our spirit to the Father in confidence. Jesus said, "Never will I leave you; never will I forsake you" (Hebrews 13:5, KJV). The fulfillment of that promise became possible at Calvary.

The Saviour went as far as death to prove His love for His children. How fitting that the women illustrated their love for Him by staying close to the cross.

In the Bible, the strongest image found to express God's love was that of a mother's love. The Hebrew word for womb was *rechem*. From this root came the most meaningful words for love in the Hebrew language: *rachamim* (tender mercy) and *racham*, the verb "to love." The root model for God's own love—which describes His very essence—was taken from the womblike love of a mother. Isaiah used this analogy in Isaiah 49:15.

The cross became the crux of history. The salvation of those living and dying before Calvary worked as a credit card. In faith, they could draw on the promises of God yet to be fulfilled. For us, salvation is a blank check through the cross. God's promises are mine in Christ Jesus. They are like a blank check I can use anytime, anywhere, by faith.

When the Father heard the words "It is finished" from His beloved Son's lips, He raised to His full height, then rolled up His sleeves and announced, "Now, I'm in charge." A shout of victory burst from the angel throng. The rest of the universe shouted as well. The rafters of heaven rang as they'd never rung before. With one sweep

from His merciful pen, He wrote across your debt of sin
and mine,
    Mission accomplished!
    Sacrifice accepted,
    Law met,
    Redeemed,
    Reconciled,
    No reprisals,
    No revenge,
    Paid in full!

# FACE TO FACE WITH FORGIVENESS

# Section
# 6

# Mary, the Ordained

# CHAPTER TWENTY-FIVE

# WHO STOLE MY JESUS?

*" 'They have taken my Lord away,' she said, 'and I don't know where they have put Him' "*
(John 20:13, NIV).

In the after-Christmas sales a couple of years ago, I found a rustic crèche with each of the nativity characters made of bisque china. I decided to replace our twenty-five-year-old plastic set I had at home, since, over the years, my daughters had worn off the paint of most of the pieces. As I inspected the china for chips and scratches, I discovered that the Jesus figure was missing.

"Where's the Jesus?" I asked as I searched the protective wrapping. But I could not find the infant figure. Taking the set to the manager, I said, "Someone stole your Baby Jesus." I asked him if the price on the nativity set could be knocked down since such a vital piece was missing. He frowned and shook his head. I argued that without the Baby Jesus, the entire crèche was meaningless. No one would want to buy it for full price.

He cocked his head to one side. "You would."

He had a point, but so did I. The nativity scene is just wood, porcelain, and hay—no different than any other pieces of wood, glass, or straw—without the Baby Jesus.

So it is with Calvary and the cross. Without the living Jesus, they are only a mound of dirt and a sliver of wood, a monument to the cruelty of man.

The soldiers rolled that heavy boulder across the entrance to Joseph of Arimathea's tomb, sealing the dead, limp body of Christ inside. If that battered body was any body but the Son of God, it might have been discovered only recently and proclaimed to be the greatest archaeological find of our century. And if the body found inside the tomb could be proven to be Jesus of Nazareth, our Lord would be just another wise teacher, another guru.

But that was not to be. The world had enough gurus, enough pretenders to the throne of God. Only the risen Lord could meet the requirements necessary for the eradication of our sins. Anyone less would fail.

During the Sabbath hours, Mary had time to contemplate all the things Jesus had said about His death and resurrection. The conflict between her faith and what others considered to be the hard core of reality befuddled her mind.

There was no time to anoint Jesus' body for burial before Sabbath on Friday. At sunset on Saturday, Mary or one of the others must have purchased the oils and spices necessary for the task. The next morning before dawn, Mary and the other women came to the tomb and found the boulder blocking the entrance rolled back and the grave empty. Mary threw her hands in the air and exclaimed, "Hallelujah! My Lord is risen, just as He said He would!"

Right?

Wrong. That's what Mary would have said had she fully understood and believed the Saviour's predictions. How interesting that the priests and Pharisees better understood His prophecies than did His followers. They're the ones who insisted that a stone be placed at the mouth of the tomb to insure the body's internment and that a contingent of soldiers stand guard in order to fend off a hoax perpetrated by the disciples.

The angels didn't roll back the stone so Jesus could get out. They removed the seal so Mary, Peter, and John could get into the tomb. This truth makes all the difference. When He arose from the dead, Jesus didn't depend on any power but His own divine power. He'd lived for thirty-three years limited by His humanity, not using His divine attributes, but calling on the same powers available to His disciples.

"He's gone! Somebody stole my Jesus!" Mary leapt to the human conclusion. *Who would do such a thing*, she wondered.

When you've confronted a problem, have you ever played Mary? Have you leapt to the obvious conclusion only to later discover a totally different explanation? I discovered my amazing agility of leaping to erroneous conclusions when I mothered 165 girls in a boarding high school situation. The gravest errors I made as a girls' dean came from jumping to conclusions.

My first "track and field" award came when during the first week on the job, I discovered a girl missing at bed check time. This girl had been displaying all the symptoms of homesickness. I figured she must have run away. I beat myself for knowing of her plight and doing nothing.

My resident assistants and I scoured the entire dormitory for our lost "lamb," with no luck. When I called the principal at an unearthly hour to report the missing girl, he told me to notify her parents. I had just done so, working hard to explain through the mother's hysteria that her daughter was missing when the missing girl, wrapped in a quilt, staggered sleepy-eyed into my office.

Wanting to be alone, she'd slipped into one of the storage rooms and curled up on the top of a stack of mattresses. By leaping to a conclusion, I had panicked everyone within reach. I only wish that I had learned my lesson. But no, I continue to be one of the best "leapers" around.

"Somebody stole my Jesus!" Mary's leap in logic didn't take into account the divine. Alarmed, Mary ran back to the city, down the still silent early morning streets, and up the stone steps to where the disciples were staying. Her fists pounded on the heavy oak door, locked from the inside. "Peter! Peter! Hurry! Open up! Jesus is gone!"

The door opened a crack; only Peter's hook nose and left eye peered between the door and the jamb. "Mary! What are you doing here at this hour? Get in here!" He opened the door, reached out and snagged her inside, then latched the door behind her. "Did anyone see you? Any soldiers? Temple police?" She shook her head.

"Now, what are you babbling about?"

"Peter, I went to the tomb to anoint the Saviour's body."

"That was foolish, woman. You wouldn't be able to remove the stone."

"That's just it, Peter, the stone was rolled back, and the tomb was empty. Someone stole my Jesus!"

"Empty? No body?" Peter stared in disbelief at the woman. Questioning whether he should give credence to the testimony of a mere woman, he asked, "Are you sure? Are you very sure?"

Mary sighed with irritation. "Yes, I'm sure."

"Maybe you went to the wrong sepulcher."

She shook her head. "I was there when they buried Him, remember?" Her words stung the guilt-ridden Peter. Would he forever feel the guilt of running when His Lord needed Him most?

"I know what I saw, Peter!" Mary's lower jaw hardened.

He cleared his throat and called to John. After a hasty appraisal of Mary's message, the two men threw on their outer garments and charged from the house. Mary followed as best she could, but she was no match for the agile fishermen.

By the time she arrived at the garden, the two men were nowhere in sight. Near the mouth of the empty tomb, she stumbled to a rock and sat down to rest. Her head ached from the tears she had shed over the tragedy of the weekend. Even in her lowest moments of sin, she'd never experienced such pain, such emptiness, such hopelessness. Her heart had broken at the foot of the cross and now, to find the Saviour's tomb empty, the final blow wreaked havoc on her soul.

# CHAPTER TWENTY-SIX

# "MASTER?"

*" 'Why are you crying?*
*Who is it you are looking for?' "*
(John 20:15, NIV).

With the shock of not finding the body of Jesus, Mary stood in front of the tomb, overwhelmed. She knew she could rule out tomb robbers. The shroud that had wrapped Jesus' body lay neatly folded on the ground. The head covering was rolled in a place by itself. No tomb robbers would have taken the time to unwrap the body and leave everything so neat, she reasoned.

She bent down to look inside once again. Two beings wearing bright robes sat inside, one at the head and one at the foot where Jesus had lain. "Why are you weeping?" one of them asked.

Distraught, Mary babbled, "Because someone has taken away my Lord and I don't know where they've put Him."

Mary stood poised at the brink of darkest despair, a place where all hope has died, where grief blinds the soul and deadens the spirit. It is the place where the reality of Jesus disappears into hellish depression.

Think of the emotional roller coaster Mary had been on! Only a short time before, her only brother had died and was resurrected after four days. Then she'd humiliated herself before the people who meant so much to her, only to be exalted by the One who meant the most to her. After the triumphant parade into Jerusalem and the bumpy week that followed, culminating with the death of her Lord, her emotional strength equaled a wrung-out dishrag. From a woman's perspective, Mary needed to find a big rock, sit down, and have a good cry.

Her eyes glazed with tears. She turned around and saw a Man dressed simply, like a gardener. Imagine the risen Lord, dressed like a gardener!

Today that would include blue jeans, a denim shirt, and a red handkerchief rolled and tied around his forehead to fend off beads of sweat. He could have worn the celestial garb of heavenly royalty, but He chose the everyday garments of His people. The newly risen Saviour said, "Woman, why are you weeping? Whom do you seek?"

You know the story. She begged for the Lord's body. "I'll take care of Him." Her love for her Saviour filled every word.

Then Jesus called, "Mary . . ."

"*Mary.*" No one could say Mary like the Master. No one. Instantly, she recognized His voice.

"Rabboni," she gasped, instantly falling to His feet in worship. How characteristic of Mary, to fall at His feet. She fell at His feet in the temple when He forgave her sins, she sat at His feet to listen, she knelt at His feet to anoint Him, and she waited at the foot of the cross while He died.

When Jesus spoke of being the good shepherd, He said, "My sheep hear my voice." Mary knew her Saviour. There was no doubt. All the confusion clouding her mind cleared instantly, like a Santa Ana wind blowing the Los Angeles smog into the sea. He reached through her veil of tears and pulled her back from the brink of hopelessness.

God calls to His children today, and they recognize His voice. And one day, in a similar setting, a sleeping Mary will hear her Lord's voice calling her from her rest, and she will immediately reply, "Rabboni?" She will know His voice on that resurrection day just as she did in the garden. For no one can say "Mary" as Jesus says "Mary."

One day, asleep in Him or awake, my Saviour will call my name, and I will recognize His voice. I will answer, "Rabboni." For no one can say "Kay" like my Jesus can say "Kay."

When He calls your name, will you recognize His voice? You will, if, like Mary, you've spent time at the Lord's feet, listening to Him and loving Him.

Jesus had instructions for Mary. "Go and tell . . ." I imagine the last thing Mary wanted to do was leave her Saviour's side, even to carry the greatest news the world would ever know.

"Go and tell? Me, Lord? You want me to go and tell? But, I'm a mere woman. Who will listen to what I have to say? I'd be too embarrassed. They'll think I'm crazy. Surely, you don't mean me."

No, this wasn't a test of Mary's loyalty and courage.

## *"Master?"*

For Mary, when the risen Saviour said "Go and tell," there would be no hesitation, no pause to "count the cost," no questioning her own abilities. Not even any worrying about how her message would be received. She went and told the greatest news in history.

Running, stumbling, tripping over rocks in her path, Mary didn't feel any exhaustion or pain. All she could think of was "He's alive! He's alive! My Jesus is alive."

People must have stared as the crazed Mary ran through the dusty alleyways of Jerusalem to reach the upper room where the disciples were hiding out. Proper women didn't run in the privacy of their homes, let alone in full view of strangers.

But Mary wasn't a proper woman—she was God's woman. And the news her Lord had given her to tell was too important to be restricted by the customs and niceties of Jewish society.

Despite the fact she'd run all the way from the cemetery, Mary flew up the stairs, two at a time. Out of breath, she pounded on the massive oak door guarding the upper room. The door opened an inch. A suspicious eye greeted her.

"He's alive! He's alive!" Tears mixed with laughter as she pushed the door open. The door slammed against the wall. She swept into the room, oblivious to the horror on the faces of the cowering disciples. "He's alive! Jesus is alive! I saw Him. I talked with Him! I tell you He's alive!"

One of the disciples grabbed her arm. "Woman, get ahold of yourself."

Another said, "Her grief has driven her over the edge."

Whirling out of her captor's reach, she shouts her news again. "No, no! I saw Him. He is alive, I tell you! He is alive. He told me to tell you the good news. He's risen from the dead and He's alive! Just as He promised."

What a privilege. What an honor! To be chosen as the one who first announces the good news of Jesus' resurrection. The Lord could have chosen Peter. He could have chosen John. But He chose Mary. Theologians believe that the unique message became Mary's because of her enormous love for her Saviour. Mary's love most represented the kind of passionate relationship God wants to have with His children. And she best understood the message of salvation. For, as Jesus said, "She who has been forgiven much, loves much."

Mary had become a woman of spiritual insights, sitting at His feet and listening to His words. Mary knew Him as a prophet. She exalted Him as a King. She turned a supper into a sacrament with her love. Mary represents the perfect disciple because she understood that Jesus was willing to die for His people. And divine poetry was written in the prose of her devotion. She became beautiful in motive, abandoning self and guilt in devotion. She understood His power and His kingdom more than did any of His other disciples.

"When the woman saw that the fruit of the tree was good for food . . . she took some and ate it" (Genesis 3:6, NIV). Long ago, in the beginning, Eve ate a piece of fruit from the forbidden tree and lost paradise. Adam also ate of the tree and lost paradise as well. But at the cross, the Saviour forgave their sins and deleted the file from heaven's hard drive.

Mary of Bethany, along with all women born since Eve, knelt at Calvary. And the Lord, who died for Adam's sin, the same Saviour who suffered for Eve's sins, did so for Mary's and Martha's and Elizabeth's and Kay's. Jesus said, "I will forgive their iniquity, and I will remember their sin no more" (Jeremiah 31:34, KJV).

Mary's story brings hope to the most guilt-ridden sinner, male or female. No matter what you do or what you've done or where your sin has taken you, sweet forgiveness is yours through the blood of Jesus Christ. For that reason, wherever the gospel of Jesus Christ is preached, Mary's story will be told. Complete surrender plus complete forgiveness equals complete love and devotion.

Don't wait another minute. Stand with Mary, face to face with Forgiveness. Like Mary, you will be astounded by the love you see there, the love Jesus has for you personally. You may not have the burdens or guilt that Mary did. But if something in your heart is holding you back from being the child of God you want to be, then stop and look deeply into Jesus' eyes.

The love you see there will change your whole world.